"Hey, Scarface!"

D.G. shot up and fixed his eyes on Chuck. Everyone scrambled to their feet. Everett dropped to the first floor of the tree fort and retrieved his slingshot. On the ground in seconds, D.G. straddled a log in front of the tree fort. Everett followed. "What do you want, Chuck?" D.G. asked.

"Who do you think you are, building a tree house in these woods?" called Chuck. "These are our woods."

Anger gripped Everett's stomach, but D.G. simply said, "Right, and I suppose Tina's pool is your pool and the United States government is . . ."

"Don't go sassing me," Chuck answered. "I'll bust you quick, Scarface." The other boys with him laughed.

"Chuck, why can't we just get along," D.G. suddenly said. "You could build your own tree fort down here if . . ."

"Don't want a tree fort," Chuck said, and spat on the ground in front of D.G.

After a moment's hesitation, Everett hurried over to D.G. He thought maybe he could yank D.G. back to safety.

"Look," D.G. said with a little shrug, "you want to make a deal, let's make a deal. We don't have to be nasty to each . . ."

"I'll be any way I want with you. Got it, Frankl?"

Chariot Books™
David C. Cook Publishing Co.

Chariot Books™ is an imprint of David C. Cook Publishing Co.
David C. Cook Publishing Co., Elgin, Illinois 60120
David C. Cook Publishing Co., Weston, Ontario
Nova Distribution Ltd., Newton Abbot, England

Cover design by Bill Paetzold
Cover illustration by Nathan Greene
First Printing, 1993
Printed in the United States of America
97 96 95 94 93   5 4 3 2 1

Library of Congress Cataloging-in-Publication Data
Littleton, Mark R.
Tree fort wars/by Mark Littleton.
p. cm.
Summary: When Chuck's prejudice against D.G., who is Jewish, threatens to lead to a fight, Everett turns to God for help.
ISBN 1-55513-764-4
[1. Prejudices—Fiction. 2. Bullies—Fiction. 3. Christian life—fiction.] I. Title
PZ7.L7364Tr 1993
[Fic]—dc20
92-44181
CIP
AC

Contents

1
The Search

Today we find the place for the tree fort," Everett Abels murmured excitedly to himself as he ran down the hill toward Rocky Creek and the rope swing.

Linc and Tina Watterson already stood at the swing, jerking the rope as they prepared to cross the creek. The sun glinted through the trees like millions of tiny mirrors. In the morning light—it was only 8:30—Linc and Tina's reddish blond hair shone like two small torches.

As Everett ran up, Tina asked in her slightly husky voice, "Where's D.G.?"

"Coming," Everett said.

"Want to swing across?" Linc asked, putting his hands in the pockets of his tennis shorts. He wore a yellow short-sleeved shirt. Though they were twins, Linc and Tina never dressed alike. Tina wore a flowered halter top and a pair of jeans shorts with a white belt.

"Better wait for D.G.," Everett said as he stopped and peered up at the branch the swing hung from. He took the end from where Linc had notched into the tree and pulled it back. The thick oaken branch creaked in the slight breeze.

Moments later, D.G. careened around the side of the Wattersons' house, wearing his blue hiking pack. He waved exuberantly as he ran. In the sunlight his reddish purple birthmark seemed to spring out. It was splotched across his left cheek like a splat from a water balloon.

"Think he brought some cupcakes?" Linc asked, licking his lips.

"Always thinking about your stomach," Tina remarked with a laugh.

But Everett answered, "Of course. D.G. doesn't travel without decent food."

They chuckled as D.G. ran up. His curly brown hair riffled in the slight air. Spiky tufts shot out from the uncombable patch. If he wasn't so smart, most people would think him an idiot the way he looked sometimes. "Ready for the search?" he said.

"Definitely," Everett said, echoing D.G.'s confident kind of talk. Linc and Tina shook their heads eagerly.

"You bring any cupcakes?" Linc asked, shifting from foot to foot like some sprinter getting ready for a hundred-yard dash.

D.G. nodded. "Three brands. Eight packs this time. My dad's stocking up now that he knows we have a regular order." He grinned and swung his hiking pack off, then knelt down and opened it. He dumped four packs out onto the ground. "Take your pick. I knew you all probably saved room from breakfast."

After the others chose, D.G. took the last pack of chocolate cupcakes. Everett watched as D.G. bit into the sweet cupcake upside down. His trademark. "To get the most of the flavor," he always said.

Everett smiled as he tongued the jelly out of its notch in a jelly krimpet. D.G. eyed them all over the edge of the cupcake. "Any of you guys ever heard of the Jersey Buckwolf?"

Linc and Tina shook their heads, but Everett looked up. "Yeah, it's an old story around New Castleton."

"I heard Seth talk about it once," D.G. said. "So I checked it out. Seems like it's a big thing here in South Jersey."

Swallowing some cupcake, Everett added, "Chuck is really into it. He used to collect news clippings and stuff."

D.G. gave him an unbelieving look. "Chuck is into the Jersey Buckwolf?"

Shrugging, Everett said, "His father, too. I guess it's kind of a hobby. It's just a myth, like the Abominable Snowman or something. But some people really believe it. How come you're interested?"

"There was something in the paper a few weeks ago," D.G. said, picking up his pack. "Then on the way down here I remembered. You know, going into the woods and all. Maybe he's out there!"

Tina sucked air noisily. "Now let's not scare each other again, D.G."

Scowling, Everett said, "It's just a story, D.G. You know that."

"Do I?" D.G. said, raising his eyebrows.

Everyone stared at him.

"It is a myth, isn't it?" Tina asked nervously.

D.G. said, "I know. But it's a fun myth. Anyway . . ."

"We're going to build a tree fort," Linc suddenly said. "We don't need to worry about any Jersey Buckwolf or whatever it is."

D.G. finished his cupcake. "Of course. Just getting you ready for true danger!" He grinned and tucked the cupcake wrapping back into his pack and then held it out for everyone. "Not supposed to litter," he said and looked at the rope.

Peering across the creek, Everett flicked his blond hair across his forehead. "So what should we look for—a big tree in the middle of the woods?"

"There won't be any big enough," D.G. answered. He chewed his upper lip a moment, then said, "This is a pretty young forest. So I think we should just find four trees together. In a little square. That way, we can build the fort straight up. Maybe even have four or five floors."

Everett wondered how D.G. knew this was a "young" forest. But D.G. was always coming out with statements like that. It wasn't that he was trying to show off—he just knew a lot of things, and he was always telling what he knew without trying to prove anything. Everett honestly thought it was great. One of D.G.'s goals was reading the *Encyclopedia Britannica* straight through by the time he reached twelfth grade. He had been at it over a year now and had already gotten past the Bs.

Everett hadn't thought about how they would build the tree fort. He remembered seeing a movie called "Swiss Family Robinson" where the shipwrecked family erected this incredible tree house with all sorts of floors, rooms, hammocks, and even a pump organ. But now he realized that was just movie stuff.

He figured there were plenty of trees that might qualify as a foursome perfect for the kind of fort they wanted to build. They wouldn't want to build the fort in the swampy places, with skunk cabbage, the rank smell of stagnant water, and mosquitoes all over the place. They'd probably go for the higher ground nearer to Seth Williamson's place. Seth was a construction worker who lived in a cabin on the other side of the wood and had the two greatest dogs on earth, two Dobermans named Whip and Bump.

The group waited as D.G. took the rope. "Last one over has to eat a mosquito sandwich." He swung across, landed nimbly on the other side, then shot the rope back. Everett handed it to Tina. "I like mosquito sandwiches more than you."

She grinned, said, "Have a nice lunch," then took the rope and swept across, skimming her sneaker on the water like a water-skier. When everyone was across, D.G. wandered off down the trail and the other three followed, meandering around through the trees on no particular path. The ground was squishy and stank, sending out little jets of brackish water as they stepped on it. But the farther away they moved from the creek, the drier it was.

Here and there they found two appropriate trees together and in one place even three in a nice triangle. But there wasn't anything in a foursome. They moved past the swampy areas up onto some higher ground.

Then Everett spotted it. They were in a little clearing. A brook that fed into the creek rambled along behind it. "Hey, look. There's four."

They ran over and measured it with their eyes, up and down. "Perfect," D.G. said. "This is it."

D.G. began explaining how they could build the fort, with the first platform about eight feet up. He had a high-pitched voice, but not whiny or girlish or nasal. He always spoke smoothly, as though he'd prepared beforehand for a speech.

He peered around at the woods and said, "There's plenty of timber here to use, and maybe we can get some good floorboarding from over at the building sites.

That way we can make it flat."

Everett noticed the bump-bump of his heart as they sized up their project for the next month. Though he had imagined more of a cabin kind of fort, the idea of platforms up in the trees actually sounded good.

After surveying the site, D.G. said, "We need to scout around before we build. We don't want anyone finding it too easily."

"Who might find it?" Tina asked. "This is pretty far back."

With a little shrug, D.G. started off and motioned for Linc to follow. "Ev and Tina can go down by the creek. Linc and I'll go up toward the other side of the development. Meet back here in say . . ." he looked at his watch, "thirty minutes."

"But who?" Tina asked, folding her arms and refusing to budge.

"The Jersey Buckwolf, for instance," D.G. said with a big grin.

Rolling her eyes, Tina said, "Leave it to D.G. to get onto something that gives me the shivers."

"It's just an old story, Teen," Everett said, chuckling. But the woods often gave him an eerie feeling. The Jersey Buckwolf might be a myth. But there were other dangers here, things you didn't think of till they jumped into your path and growled. Then there were people. The TV was always brimming with news about some weirdo, murderer, or drug gang. They didn't need that.

Still, the quiet of the woods and the dank smell of stagnant water was somehow assuring. If anyone came back here, it was just for a hike. No one would want to live back here for good.

After watching D.G. and Linc trot off toward the hilly areas to the south of Rocky Creek, Tina and Everett walked downwind in the opposite direction. In a minute they reached the water and followed it away from the houses.

Tina looked around at the trees. "We did a leaf project in school last year. Had to identify leaves of all the trees. D.G. knows them all, doesn't he? He seems to be a real woodsman."

Everett chuckled. "D.G. seems to be a real everything." They sauntered along, but it was all woods. In ten minutes they turned to go back.

When they reached the four trees, neither D.G. nor Linc were to be seen. They sat down with their backs against one of the trees. Everett pulled a sliver of grass and put it in his mouth.

"Yuck," said Tina. "Why do boys always do that?"

"Do what?"

"Pull out grass and put it in their mouths."

"What's the matter? Don't girls do that?"

Tina shook her head. "No way."

"How come?"

"I don't know," Tina said, smoothing the grass with her hand. "Why don't boys polish their nails?"

Snorting dramatically, Everett joked, "We chew them. We don't paint them."

"Hah!" said Tina. "That figures."

Everett liked the talk. Tina was all right. Then in the woods behind them, a branch snapped. They turned lazily to see if it was D.G. and Linc, expecting that it would be. But it wasn't. D.G. would be running a monologue as he walked. And he would be more careful. No snapped sticks with D.G.

Whoever it was wasn't talking.

Both Tina and Everett instinctively hunched down and listened. More sticks snapped and leaves rustled. Someone moved toward them through the east woods, from near the creek.

Everett touched Tina's shoulder and whispered, "We'd better get out of sight. I don't think we ought to be seen."

They crawled behind a log with a hump of moss on the top and peered over one of the stumpy branches.

A moment later two boys walked into the clearing. It was Chuck Davis and Stuart Coble, two kids from up the street. Everett was mildly surprised, since he hadn't seen them in the woods lately. They both had hatchets on their belts and bowie knives.

Neither of the boys looked in a friendly mood. Chuck's sandy-colored hair stuck out from under a red Phillies cap. He wore a black T-shirt. Stuart was shorter than Chuck, with straight, dark hair. He wore no hat, and was thin and wiry, while Chuck was thick and muscular, even for a twelve year old.

"Isn't nothin' here," Stuart said. "They probably aren't back here today."

Chuck said, "They're here somewhere. That Jew Frankl always has them doing something." His voice, dripping with sarcasm and anger, made Everett's back prickle.

Tina whispered, "He still acts awful about everything."

"I know," Everett said. "We'd better lay low. We don't need a problem now."

Whining in his nasal voice, Stuart said, "Well, let's just sit down. We've been walking around for hours. It smells like skunk down here."

"Yeah, I wanna suck on a butt, anyway. Want one?"

Everett watched with amazement as Chuck pulled out a pack of cigarettes and lit up. He knew Chuck smoked sometimes, but now it appeared it had become a habit.

As the two boys talked quietly, Chuck began telling Stuart that they couldn't let anyone mess around with their woods. "I don't want Frankl hanging around down here. He stinks the place up. That's why it smells all the time."

Stuart seemed a lot less defensive. "They're not a bunch of wimps. You know what they did at the house," he reminded Chuck, referring to a fight earlier in the summer.

"Pure luck," Chuck said. "Everett was just lucky. But I don't care about him anymore. Frankl has his mind now, the way his kind get people's minds. Like my grandfather says." Chuck whipped out his hatchet, held it over his head, then threw it fiercely against a tree trunk. It bounced off into the brush. Chuck walked over and picked it up. Then he cut a slice out of the tree.

A few minutes later, the two got up and walked back the way they'd come in. Both Everett and Tina began to breathe easier.

3 Hope and Fear

"I don't like him at all anymore," said Everett. "Smoking cigarettes now? Acts like some hood or something."

Tina peered toward the right where D.G. and Linc had gone. "It's a good thing D.G. wasn't around. Did you hear what he said? How can anyone talk like that? D.G. is such a great kid."

Everett sighed and tried to see where they were going. But the woods swallowed them up. "Well, at least they didn't see us."

The air was warmer now, and Everett noticed he was

sweating, partly from tension. Tina squinted off through the woods. She said, "I guess they're gone."

"Not for long," Everett answered, telling himself to be calm.

Tina was quiet. Then, "I guess it's never over with some people, is it?"

"I guess not."

"You don't think he'd actually use that hatchet on someone, do you?" Tina voice was a raspy whisper. "That would be murder."

"No," Everett said with a sigh. "Chuck is a lot of talk. He has to act big. Like there are a bunch of people watching him or something. I think he probably even acts big when he lies down to go to sleep."

Tina chuckled. "At least we can laugh about him."

"Maybe," Everett said quietly. "We'll just have to avoid him. We don't need to get into another fight."

They waited and listened some more, then stood up. Tina said, "Where are Linc and D.G.? I still feel a little scared, actually."

"They'll be back." Everett tried to sound like D.G.—confident and in control. He glanced at Tina. "Don't worry. I wouldn't let him touch you."

The moment he said it, he felt embarrassed, but Tina smiled. "I know. I always feel safe with you and Linc and D.G."

They stood listening and waiting, still crouched behind the tree and not saying much. Everett could tell Tina didn't like being there, but he was sure she wasn't going to chicken and run.

Ten minutes later, D.G. and Linc swaggered into the clearing. D.G. was full of jokes and happy. "No houses for several hundred yards, I'd say. People must have known we'd already claimed it. This will be the perfect place."

After a quick glance at Tina, Everett told them about Chuck and Stuart. He didn't mention what Chuck had said about Jews.

They listened without comment, then Linc said, "We can take him."

But D.G. said, "He's just jealous. It's nothing to worry about. Brains over brawn, remember? And anyway, maybe we can win him over with some cupcakes."

Feeling less than confident, Everett said, "It won't be that easy, D.G."

The smaller boy shrugged. "You can't go through life being mean to people because they're mean to you. We can be decent to him. If he forces us, we'll fight back. But as long as he doesn't know we're here, we're safe." D.G. stared at the group. "Hey, if it's me he wants, then let him come to the door like the rest of my fans. I'll give him an autograph, just like anyone else."

Everyone laughed, and it made Everett feel better that D.G. wasn't angry. But he remembered how D.G. always said that you don't have to return fire with fire. Sometimes you can return fire with humor and it works. Still, he wondered if Chuck was even capable of joking about it.

Finally, D.G. sighed, "Come on, let's get back to the kibbutz. We need to have some lox, bagels, and cream cheese. That'll make us feel more David-like."

"What?" said Linc. He was looking at his muscles, craning his neck around from left to right. Everett figured he was trying to decide which arm had the bigger muscles.

D.G. joked again in Linc's direction, "If you weren't always trying to be Arnold Schwartzenegger, you'd know something." He explained about kibbutz being a settlement in Israel and lox being salmon—and how it makes a great sandwich with bagels and cream cheese. Everyone knew about David and Goliath from the Bible.

They followed D.G. to the rope and swung across the creek. When they reached the back of the Wattersons' house, D.G. said, "The first thing we need to do is get some building tools. Axes. Hammers. Nails. Saws. All the stuff for building the fort. See what you can dig up, and we'll meet back here tomorrow."

They all parted, but Tina touched Everett's arm after D.G. hurried off. "You don't think Chuck will be a problem, do you?"

"Yeah, I think he will," Everett said soberly. "But D.G.'s right, maybe we can humor Chuck out of it. There's no reason for us to be enemies anymore." He looked from Tina to Linc. For not being identical twins they looked a lot alike. They even moved their lips and noses the same way when they were frustrated.

He ran down the driveway. "See you later on."

They waved and he hurried across the street. He had to watch his younger brother and sister that afternoon, so he wouldn't be going back down to the tree fort. Looking up the road at Chuck's house, he saw it looked the same as always, green shutters, quiet. He remembered good times in the basement and playroom. What had gone wrong with Chuck? he wondered. Why couldn't they be friends? It should be easy, especially when they had once been so close. He said to himself, "Maybe I can work something out with them on my own, too."

But he wondered if any real peace was possible. Ever. How did you make peace with someone who just didn't want to?

4 Revelations

Their collection of tools the next day amounted to two saws, three hammers, two hatchets, a screwdriver (which Tina had brought and D.G. remarked that it was a nice idea but no good for building tree forts), several bags of nails, three pocketknives (D.G.'s, Linc's, and Everett's), and some rope. D.G. said they could use the rope for lashing poles to the trees, if necessary.

They tucked what they could into D.G.'s knapsack, and he hurtled over the water. In a few minutes they all stood before the trees. D.G. briefly inspected each tree. "Before we do anything," he said, "we have to mark the trees."

He opened his jackknife and carved letters in the gray bark of the biggest tree, a tall, thick ash. Everett watched as D.G. painstakingly cut D.G.F. into the bark. Tina said, "What does D.G. stand for? I forget."

D.G. gave her a wry look, then shrugged and said, "Go ahead, remind her, Everett."

About to tell her the truth, Everett suddenly smiled craftily. "I think it means Dudley Grimebrain Frankl," he said, waiting for a response.

Turning around, D.G. laughed. "That's right, except my friends just call me Grimey."

Tina rolled her eyes. "All right, I get it. But what does it really mean?"

"Well, actually," D.G. said, pursing his lips, "It means Doggone Genius."

"No, it doesn't," Linc said, catching the mood. "I hear it stands for Dobie the Grouch."

Tina folded her arms as D.G. continued his painstaking carving. "Actually, I do know what it really means."

Everyone waited.

"Donald the Guck."

They all laughed.

Finally, D.G. said. "It means Dodai Gamaliel. It is weird, I'll admit that. But you have to remember they were great names in the glory days of Israel."

"Yeah, right," said Linc as he rolled over the branch and swung down. "I bet those guys never lived their names down."

D.G. stopped carving. "And you can call me D.G., thank you."

D.G. handed the knife to Everett. "Pick a tree, Ev."

Everett walked over to smallest tree, one with gray, flaky bark, and worked at cutting the letters E.A. But the E was bigger than the A. It also ended up on a slight slant. When he finished, D.G. said, "Superb. Now Linc."

Tina interrupted. "I'm older than Linc."

Everett glanced at the two. Linc was nodding. "She was almost an hour before me. That's what Mom says."

"When were you born?" D.G. asked, licking his lips.

Tina answered, "November 30. Linc is December first. I was born five minutes before midnight. He was born at almost 1 a.m."

Standing stock still, D.G. looked from Tina to Linc and back. "So you're twins but you don't even have the same birthday? That's amazing."

Tina nodded. "It's kind of a Ripley's Believe It or Not thing."

Linc flexed a muscle. "Right, but I'm stronger."

"In odor," Tina added. She looked at Everett. "When's your birthday?"

"July 25."

"Oh, so it's coming up soon. We'll have to have a party." Tina looked at D.G.

He handed her the knife. "My birthday's January 9." He bent down to pick up a hatchet.

Everett nodded. "So you are the oldest."

D.G. cleared his throat. Giving them his mysterious

look, he said, "I'm like my mother. I never discuss my age."

Now Everett's curiosity was really struck. He homed in. "Wait a second, D.G. You're not getting out of this. Were you born the same year as us or not?"

"Well, let's see," D.G. said, wrinkling his heavy eyebrows. "Must have been somewhere between the year you were born and the year my Uncle Ezekiel had his car accident!"

Tina jabbed her knife into the tree. "Quit stalling, D.G. I bet you're younger than all of us."

D.G. bowed his head and looked up at them. His dark eyes had that sly look that always came into them when he had an idea. "Well, I just turned eleven in January."

Tina exclaimed, "So you are the youngest!"

D.G. shrugged. "Okay, now, let's get on with the real work here."

Everyone walked around and watched as Tina carved TINA in big, bold letters on the third tree, the one diagonal to Everett's. The last A had a long curlicue dangling from it. "That's a kitty tail," she said. "I always sign my name like that." She handed the knife to Linc.

Linc carved in his initials, L.A.W., then stepped back. "I'll be the law around here," he said.

The moment he said it, there was a loud bark and everyone jumped. Seconds later, Whip and Bump, the two Dobermans belonging to Seth Williamson, bounded into the clearing. Seth was a widower and construction worker they often visited who lived in a cabin on the other side of the big woods. The dogs galloped over to them, woofing and snuffling. Everett let both Bump and Whip lick him, then Whip stood up on his hind legs and put his front paws on Tina's chest. Seth's deep voice sounded from the underbrush. "What you got there, boys?"

"It's us," D.G. yelled. "Seth, it's me and Everett and Linc and Tina."

A moment later, Seth appeared in the clearing, a red bandanna on his head. He was sweaty, wearing his overalls. "Well, I'll be," he said. "Seems like I run into you little ones ever'where I go."

The four ran up to Seth, with Whip and Bump bouncing beside them. "So what you all doing in the woods? Not killin' Indians, I hope."

"We're going to build a tree fort," D.G. said excitedly, sticking out his chest.

"Tree fort!" Seth's bright blue eyes looked like jewels in his grizzled face. "Where you buildin' it?"

D.G. pointed to the trees. "Right here. Right where these four trees are. See, we can make platforms and sides and everything."

Seth said, "Well, we was just takin' a walk. We come down here now and then. Whip and Bump like scaring up rabbits and squirrels. Say, you ever been to the caves?"

D.G. nearly shouted, "There're caves around here?"

"Sure," Seth said. "I'm surprised you haven't found 'em. I used to mess around in 'em when I was a kid. We used to come back here all the time, trappin' muskrat, lookin' for deer, and the caves. I never showed you the caves?"

"No, sirree!" D.G. said. "Will you take us to them?"

"Well, come on then, you can go inside. I can't fit no more. But you can. I was just goin' that way anyway. There's a little spring, too."

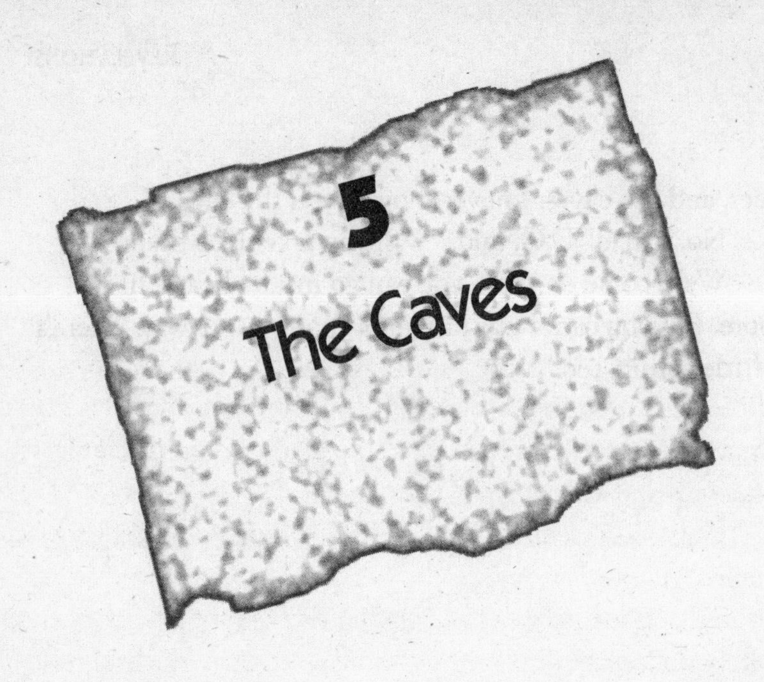

Everett, D.G., Linc, and Tina all followed Seth down the trail. As they walked, Seth talked about the woods, what he'd seen there as a child. "There was beaver here for sometime. Built a dam down aways. But they're all gone now. We seen deer all over. Bucks, does, fawns. Never shot any here, though. We went up to Pennsy for that. Didn't get my own rifle till I was fourteen. Me and Palmer, Juice, Lefty, and Smith used to come down here all the time."

"Who were they?" Everett said, keeping stride behind Seth. D.G. walked behind him, and Tina and Linc brought up the rear with the two dogs running back and forth in the woods ahead of and behind them.

"Just friends. One was killed in Korea—Smith. Lefty tried to make it in baseball, but he never got beyond the minors. I haven't seen him in years. Played first base. He hit over .350 his last three years in high school. But he took to drinkin' and burned out. Palmer I see now and then. He's a construction man like me. Sometimes we get on the same site and swap stories for a while."

"What about Juice?" D.G. asked. "How did he get that name?"

Seth shook his head and sighed. "The idiot stuck his pinky on a spark plug on a motorcycle engine. We told him he'd get hit with the juice and could be killed, but he didn't believe us. Boy, did he light up. The juice hit him like a bolt out of the blue. Turned every shade of red, orange, and green. After that we always called him Juice."

"So what happened to him?" D.G. persisted.

"Real sad story," Seth said. "He got into crime, robbed a bank, then got killed doing a store or somethin'. I read about it in the papers. He was always havin' to take a risk. Regular life wasn't exciting enough for him."

Seth wound through the woods past many points the group had seen, and soon they were climbing on a trail that led up a slope. After fifteen or twenty minutes, they reached a small mountain, more like a hill, but Seth called it Laurel Mountain. They began climbing and passing through strewn rocks cropping out from the side of the hill like lone teeth. Soon they were in among many rocks jumbled about with moss growing all over them. Trees stuck out between them but the forest had begun to thin out.

"Big rocks all over here," Seth said. "We used to play hide-and-seek, cowboys, everythin' in here. Found these caves. Let's see."

Seth stopped, pulled off his bandanna and mopped his forehead. The foursome stood around him waiting. Everett was wondering what might be in the cave. He'd only visited one, called Luray Caverns in Virginia, on a trip with his parents. Stalactites had dripped down from the ceiling and stalagmites had risen up from the floor in all kinds of shapes and colors. But he didn't think this cave would be like that.

Surveying the area, Seth suddenly pointed. "There it is—see it?"

The dogs sniffed in among the rocks, and all four kids stretched their necks to see where Seth was pointing.

"Oh, you're all blind as chickens with their heads cut off," Seth said jokingly. "Come on. You can't see it easily 'less you know what you're lookin' for."

He meandered among the rocks, and the foursome kept close behind him. The dogs raced back and forth. Everett noticed flies buzzing in the area. The wind rustled the leaves in the trees. Then Seth stopped. "Hear it?"

Everyone was quiet.

"Hear what?" D.G. asked.

"The spring. Bubbling up. Listen close now."

Everett strained to hear. "Yeah, I hear it. A little gurgling noise."

"Yeah, we hear it," Tina and Linc exclaimed together.

D.G. sniffed the air and said, "Where's it coming from?"

"Inside the cave," Seth said with a wink. "Come on this way."

They walked in among the huge rocks and then Everett saw it, an opening about two feet high and three feet wide. It was oval, almost square the way the rocks were shaped. You couldn't see it easily. Not from far away. A dribble of water came out of the mouth in the middle.

"You got to straddle it or you'll get all wet. Any of you have a flashlight?"

D.G. smiled. "Always prepared. I've got a flashlight, some matches, and even a candle."

Seth laughed. "Boy, you do come prepared. What else you got in that sack?"

"You name it—he has it," Everett said.

D.G. said, "Come on, last one in has to eat a mosquito sandwich."

He scrambled forward, but Seth reached out and grabbed him by the collar. "Wait a moment, boys. Let me check it out. Sometimes wild dogs and things start livin' in these kind of places. You better let me take a look first. Then you can go in. But I'd best be headin' back. Got some shopping and stuff to do."

"I'm not afraid of any wild dog," D.G. said.

"I know you're not," Seth said, winking at Everett and Tina. "But I'm afraid for the dog. Wouldn't want him gettin' bit by the likes of you."

"I wouldn't do that," D.G. protested.

Seth shook his head. "Just let me peek my eyes in there a second, then you can go in. Okay?"

D.G. nodded. Everyone waited breathlessly as Seth knelt down, poked his arm into the cave with D.G.'s flashlight. The water lapped at the tip of his boot as it crunched on the dirt, but the stream was only a few inches wide in a crevice in the middle of the cave, so he didn't get wet. Seth called, "Yalooooo!"

Everett heard a faint echo. Then Seth backed out. "It's all right. Nothin' in there but spiders, snakes, and probably a bat or two. But you can handle them."

D.G. bent down to look in. A moment later he disappeared into the cave. Everyone else followed. The cave was dank and musty, but the stream gave it a fresh, cool smell that reminded Everett of a garden. D.G. waved the flashlight back and forth along the narrow path. Just inside the opening, the cave widened into an igloolike area, then dipped low in the back. But the chamber obviously went back farther.

Seth crouched in the mouth of the cave and said, "It goes back to another cave a little ways around the side of the hill. But it's a good place to hide. Me and Smith and the rest of 'em had some good times here."

D.G. crept back to where the group was, and they sat in a semicircle on either side of the stream of water. After looking around at the walls, everyone crawled back out.

In the sunlight, Everett asked Seth, "Where does the

water come from? Is it okay to drink?"

"Probably not," Seth said, making a little splash at the mouth of the cave and tasting it. "Starts back deep in the hill where you can't get because the cave is too narrow. Must be a spring under the hill pushing the water up. Probably under a lot of pressure because we get so much rain around here. There may be an underground river deep down. It's always under pressure, so it pushes up. This is one of the places. There're several springs around here."

Everett bent down to taste it. D.G. followed, then Linc and Tina. After licking her lips, Tina said, "It tastes a little coppery or something."

"Minerals," Seth said.

"Mineral water," D.G. answered. "Like they sell in the store. Hey, maybe we could bottle this and sell it."

Seth laughed. "Yeah, that would be good. But who would want to buy this when you can get the good old chlorinated version from the tap at home, with fluoride in it to keep your teeth strong?"

Everett answered, "We could say it's good for your health. We could call it Miracle Water or something."

"Like Polar Spring Water or that stuff from France, Perrier," D.G. said excitedly.

"Yeah, and what happens when they want to see a miracle first?" Seth said with a grin. "Now I got to skedaddle, boys and girls."

He started off with the dogs and wound around the rocks. Everyone watched till he disappeared, then D.G.

said, "So what should we do in here?" He shone his flashlight farther back on the walls of the cave. For the first time they noticed some writing. It was faded, written in chalk. But there were some of the names Seth mentioned. "Smith and Barbara" was written on one wall with a heart around it. On the top was another saying, "Lefty—Philadelphia Phillies All-Star." On the back side they saw the saying, "Seth tells lies for fun and profit."

D.G. squinted at it and held his light on it. "What's that mean?"

Looking up at it, Tina said, "I bet it was because Seth's such a good storyteller."

Nodding, D.G. added, "I bet that was it." There was a long pause as everyone looked around at the walls. D.G. pulled out a candle and lit it. "So I don't run down the batteries on my flashlight." The candle threw great shadows onto the walls that brought on an eerie feeling.

Then Tina said, "That's what we should do here—tell stories."

"Right," Linc said. "Ghost stories."

Everett shivered. "I don't think we need to scare each other now."

"No ghost stories, but scary," Tina said. "Come on, D.G., you must have one."

The light from the mouth of the cave filtered in a bit, but the candle shone in all directions, casting dancing shadows on the walls. Everything was quiet and still except for the gurgle of the spring deep in the cave.

D.G. laughed. "I assure you, you don't want to hear one of mine."

"The scariest one you got," Linc quickly said.

A prickly rush shot through Everett and the hairs on his neck tingled.

D.G.'s eyes twinkled in the soft candlelight. His dark complexion gave him a sinister look. Everyone's eyes fixed on D.G. He squinted. "I don't want to scare you now. Not on a nice day like this."

"We won't be scared," Linc said.

"No, we want to be scared," Tina said, her eyes shining. She bared her teeth. "Tell a story about the Jersey Buckwolf." She glanced at the other two and raised her eyebrows.

"And you're the one who doesn't like scary stuff," Linc suddenly said.

Tina stuck her tongue out at him. "We can always change our minds, can't we?" She looked back at D.G. "Come on, Dodai Gamaliel. Give us your best shot."

In the cave, all remained quiet and still.

Everett leaned back against the wall, listening to the water lap on the rocks and the sound of everyone's breathing. A moment later, D.G. said, "You sure you all want to hear this?"

Tina and Linc nodded. Everett's heart pounded hard in his chest.

D.G. said slowly, "Okay, but if you run out of here screaming, don't blame me." His voice turned gravelly and dark. "Well, it's just a good thing it isn't night, because we might not get out of this one alive."

As Everett leaned back against the wall, his mouth suddenly felt dry and tingly.

6 The Jersey Buckwolf

D.G.'s voice rasped, almost like Seth's, and he spoke low and menacingly, "He's a creature, part deer, part wolf. He has antlers on his head like a buck, each one sharp as the tip of a bayonet. And he has a mouth like a wolf, long fangs, black lips. Green eyes that glow in the dark."

D.G. put his hands up to his eyes like binoculars. Everett perked up for any sounds in the back of the cave.

"Except you never see him." D.G. took down his hands. "He travels silently through the woods. You don't hear him till he comes up behind you and . . ." D.G. suddenly squeezed Tina's bare leg. She howled and jumped.

"Till he comes up and grabs you!" D.G. said.

Everyone laughed nervously.

"This is good, D.G.," Linc said. "Keep going."

With a quick nod, D.G. said, "He travels through the Pine Barrens of South Jersey. But every now and then he comes as far north as Trenton and Ocean City. And the woods around New Castleton."

"Awww," Everett said. "That's not true."

"Hush," D.G. said, putting his finger to his lips. "You have to be quiet if you want to hear."

Everett noticed the pounding at his temples. He was always amazed at how cool D.G. could be when he was telling a story like this.

"A year or so ago there were four men—scientists and hunters," D.G. said, "who wanted to stalk the Jersey Buckwolf—to prove once and for all he was a myth. They came down from North Jersey right to these woods. Two Piney women had seen something on the other side of the Pike, and the men came down here to take a look around. The Jersey Buckwolf only comes out at night, so they knew they'd have to camp out.

"The men were equipped with everything they needed—thirty-five caliber Remington rifles, powerful enough to stop a black bear. Three-fifty-seven caliber pistols. Lanterns. Traps. Tents. They wanted to catch this thing and show it to the world. But you know what?"

No one said a word. Every eye was fixed on D.G.'s face. "None of these men believed in the Jersey Buckwolf. They thought it was all a hoax. But the people in the Pines knew better. They kept their doors locked at night. They always brought in all the pets, chickens, and cattle, and they made sure their guns were loaded. They never knew when the Buckwolf might strike."

As D.G. spoke, there was a sudden scratching noise, like a fingernail running along a zipper. Everett looked at D.G.'s hands, then saw that D.G. was rubbing his nail on the zipper of his blue jeans shorts.

"When the Buckwolf comes, though, he sometimes makes a sound. Some said it was his teeth clinching and unclinching. Others said it was the claws on his front paws—wolf paws—clicking against one another as he walked. But when you heard that sound, you would freeze, just freeze with dumb fright. You knew any moment those fangs might tear into your throat or rip your heart out."

Everett gazed at the water gurgling in front of him and at the candle.

"These scientists—see—they were going to prove the Jersey Buckwolf was an impostor, some Piney man or someone who just pretended to scare people. They were going to catch him and make him confess. Their names were Wilson, Blomberg, Raushlitz, and Dobbs. All came from the state university. Real scientists."

D.G. stopped and took a breath.

"They camped out that first night on the other side of Route 70," he went on, "and saw nothing. The next day, they moved deeper into the woods on the other side of

Rocky Creek, before the housing development went up. Again, there was nothing."

After a pause, D.G. continued. "Third night out, they came down into this woods, not far from these rocks. They camped in a clearing. That night they lit a campfire and sat around it. They talked quietly into the evening, but eventually they all got tired. It was Wilson who had the first watch. So he sat up as the others went to sleep. The woods were abuzz with the sound of bugs and crickets. And then the woods grew silent. Just like it is now."

Everett noticed that even the gurgling of the water seemed to have stopped. But D.G. didn't wait.

"Then there was a noise out in the trees far beyond the tents. Just like this." There was the scratchy, clicky noise Everett had heard before. He could see D.G. doing it with his fingernail. "Just like I'm making with my nail on the zipper.

"Wilson stood up. He grabbed his three-fifty-seven pistol and touched Blomberg in the nearest sleeping bag. 'Don't wake the others,' he said. 'There's something out there. I want you to cover me.'

"Blomberg nodded, and pulled himself out of the bag. Wilson headed toward the sound. Then he saw it. Two eyes. He was sure it was the faker. He ran out toward it. Blomberg watched as he stood next to the fire. Then Wilson yelled. There was a gunshot. *BOOM*. Another. *BOOM*. Then he screamed, 'No!' His voice was cut off, just like that. Then it was dead silent."

Everyone leaned forward. Tina and Linc were breathing almost in unison.

"The other two men awakened from the shots. Blomberg yelled to them, 'Something's happened!' He grabbed his rifle and rammed in a shell. They had to go after Wilson. All of them got together. They began calling Wilson's name. 'Bud! Bud! You out there?'

"It was ice silent. They were all shaking. Blomberg said two should go, one should stay. Raushlitz said he'd stay. They turned on their flashlights and stepped out into the woods. The crickets had taken up their chirp again.

"Raushlitz waited by the fire. Then there was that eerie silence. The crickets stopped. The woods seemed to have died.

"Then he heard it behind him. *Rizza-rizza-rizz-rizz-rizz. Clickety-click*. Raushlitz whipped around. Two eyes coming straight at him. Just zooming right out of the forest. Raushlitz screamed. He tried to bring up his rifle. It was too late."

D.G. waited. Everett was so scared he could barely breath. He noticed Tina pressed up against him and Linc was sitting closer.

"The two men in the woods stopped and whipped around," D.G. said, his voice still low and dark. " 'What happened?' Blomberg said. 'Something at the fire,' Dobbs answered. 'Raushlitz screamed.' They peered through the woods at the glowing coals of the fire, but could see nothing. The woods were silent. Then there was a rustle to their left. *Clickety-click. Rizza-rizz.* Blomberg turned and fired. *BOOM. BOOM.*

"But there was nothing. It was silent again." D.G. let the tension build until Everett almost screamed for him to finish. Then he said very low and whispery, "There was another rustle to their right. *Clicka-clicka. Rizz-rizz. BOOM.* Dobbs fired. *BOOM. BOOM.* Blomberg was shooting now.

" 'What's going on?' Blomberg yelled. 'Someone's playing tricks on us,' answered Dobbs. They both began calling for Wilson and Raushlitz.

"Then they heard it again.

" 'We have to get back to the fire,' Blomberg said. 'Raushlitz may need us.'

"They walked slowly, cautiously through the woods. Then a rustle again to their left. Then another, to the right. Then the sound. *Rizz-rizz-rizza-rizz. Clickety-click.*

"*Rizz-rizz-rizz.* The men fired. *BOOM. BOOM.* They fired in every direction, their backs to one another. Then Dobbs heard Blomberg scream out, right behind him.

"Dobbs didn't even turn around. He felt the hot breath on his neck. He felt a claw touch him right at his shoulder.

"Dobbs ran. The noises filled the night. *Rizz-rizz-rizz. Clickety-click.* He felt hot breath on the back of his neck again. And those claws. He ran. He screamed as he felt a claw touch his cheek. He twisted away. Then there was something grabbing at his feet. He tripped. He slid. Water. There was water under him. And a hole. A hole in the wall. He scrambled through. He was somewhere. Inside somewhere."

D.G.'s voice was so eerie in the candlelight, Everett felt as though he was jumping out of his skin.

"Dobbs looked at the hole. There was a shaft of moonlight shining down right over the entrance. It was moonlight, beautiful moonlight. He thought maybe he was safe.

"And then this thing with antlers and bluish-green eyes appeared in the hole. It looked him directly in the eye. Dobbs knew in that moment that he was done for. He yelled at it. He told it to go away. He searched for his pistol. But he'd dropped it when he was running. He was defenseless.

"The thing crept forward."

D.G. stopped and Everett almost fell forward. Tina's fingernails dug deeply into his arm. D.G. leaned way forward, his eyes full of confidence in the candlelight. Linc's face was white. He seemed to have frozen solid.

The silence grew until it seemed to fill Everett's mind.

D.G. wiped his brow with his hand. He put the other over his head. Then Everett heard the noise.

Rizz-rizz-rizza. Clickety-click. Clickety-click.

D.G. whispered, "It's here!"

Everett jumped. They all turned around and peered down the cave. Instantly, the candlelight went out.

Clickety-click. Rizza-rizz.

D.G. yelled, "Run!"

Tina scrambled through the hole in seconds. Everett was right behind her. Then Linc. Tina sped through the rocks, down the hill. Everett's feet pounded behind her. Everyone else followed. Everett's heart seemed to be in his mouth. When they reached the bottom, Tina stopped and turned around, pulling out her slingshot. In the light, Everett noticed the birds singing. They all stopped together under a tree, panting.

"Where's D.G.?" Linc asked. His voice shook.

They looked up the hill.

D.G. emerged slowly from the hole and hurried down to them.

"What was it? Was it in there?" Tina cried.

"A made-up Buckwolf!" D.G. said.

As they stood there, everyone laughed. The sunshine shone around them.

D.G. pointed to his head. "Plumb crazy." He looked seriously from face to face, his eyes boring into them. Then he laughed.

They all laughed together. "You really had me going," Tina said.

"Me, too," answered Linc. "Where did you get that story, D.G.?"

The boy shrugged. "Between reading books, watching movies, keeping up with the news, and having a nightmare now and then, I guess it just came up out of my brain."

"That was great!" Everett exclaimed, slapping D.G. on the back.

"So it's not true," Tina said.

"Not a word of it," D.G. assured her. Then he added, "Oh, no, I left everything in the cave. We'll have to go back."

"You go back," Tina said. "I'll guard the entrance."

They all chuckled again and D.G. quickly retrieved his backpack and the candle. As they walked back through the woods, Linc said, "One thing's for sure, I'm not going in that cave at night alone. Ever. Even if it is just a story."

When they reached the trees the next morning, D.G. said, "Okay, now we begin building. The way I see it is this." He explained how they should build the fort in two tiers or platforms about five feet apart. They would make the first floor about seven or eight feet up. They would get to it by a rope ladder they would have to make.

"We need four thicker trees, fairly straight, to start putting up the first floor," said D.G. "Let's see if we can find some." He eyed the four trees, then walked over to them, stretching out his arms to measure the distance between them. "I'd say we'll need a good eight feet for each runner.

They shouldn't be more than three or four inches in diameter."

He turned and stared at the three others. D.G. was always thinking a mile ahead of everyone else, but Everett wondered if everyone else knew what he was talking about. He wasn't sure himself. It had been a long explanation. Linc was rubbing his nose. Tina was playing with her hair. He thought maybe everyone had become a little confused.

Suddenly, D.G. stared at them. "What—did someone give each one of you a frontal lobotomy?"

Everett forced himself to jump up. But once he was standing, he felt ready to begin. "I'm ready to go, Captain. I'm going to find a straight tree at least eight feet long, no more than three inches thick."

Tina giggled.

D.G. turned to them. "Let's hop to it. We don't have all morning."

Everett stooped down to pick up a saw. Linc took the hatchet.

"What do you want me to do?" asked Tina.

"Look around for some straight trees we can use as floorboards," said D.G. "I think we passed some down in that direction." He pointed to the south, away from the creek. "But watch out for that Jersey Buckwolf thing. We don't want to run into him." He twitched his eyebrows with a look of mock terror on his face.

Tina shook her head. "Don't you remember? He only comes out at night. And anyway, he's probably more afraid of what you're telling people about him than of anything else."

Smiling over her joke, Tina started off downstream. Linc called after her, "You're going alone?"

"Unless someone wants to join me," said Tina.

Everett waited. But D.G. said, "Why don't you go with her, Ev? Even if she's in our army, she's still a girl."

Immediately, Tina turned and stuck out her tongue, wrinkled up her face, and then swaggered off. Everett followed her, not trying particularly hard to keep up.

In a short time, they found a grove of long, straight poplars, anywhere from two to four inches thick. Everett placed the crosscut saw against the trunk low to the ground. Several skunk cabbages grew around the base, and when he squashed one with his foot, a rank odor wafted into the air.

"Yuck," Tina cried, "did you have to do that?"

"Scares away the Jersey Buckwolf," Everett countered. She rolled her eyes.

They sawed three trees down and cut off all the branches, stripping them until each trunk was long and smooth. Then they bundled them with the piece of rope Tina had carried. The creek sputtered and foamed over a shallow area nearby. After forty-five minutes, sweating and hot, Everett suggested they soak their feet. In less than a minute they had their sneakers off and waded into the four-inch-deep water on a small shoal of rocks. Tina knelt down and cleaned her hands in the water. A bit of sap had oozed out of the trees onto their fingers.

"Do you think D.G.'s really reading the encyclopedia?" she asked, giving Everett a sidelong glance.

"If he skipped second grade, he's probably some kind of genius. He seems awful smart to me."

"Yeah, but do you think he really skipped?"

"Why would he lie to us?"

Tina pursed her lips and wrinkled her nose. "This water smells a little. Do you think it's polluted?"

"My mom says not to walk in it. But it's clear."

"Well, I'm definitely not drinking it."

Everett ran his fingers over the stones on the bottom as he crouched over the water. The creek was cool and tugged at his ankles. It felt good. "Too bad so many streams are polluted today. My dad's always telling me about when he was a kid how he used to go swimming in the river—not around here, but above Philadelphia where he grew up."

"My dad is buying us little boats for the pool."

"Oh, is the pool filled up yet? I didn't notice."

"Next week. Then we can all swim. Take breaks from building the fort." Tina squinted at him.

Everett looked down into the water at all the stones. They were brown, tan, white, speckled, black, red. He thought it would be great if they were jewels. They'd be rich.

A voice suddenly rang out behind them, "Hey, you're supposed to be working."

Everett and Tina whipped around. D.G. and Linc stood on the edge of the woods looking down on them. Everett stood up and Tina threw her braid over her shoulder. "We were just washing off," she said.

"Well, come on. We've got a long way to go," D.G. said.

8
Pacts and Problems

The foursome worked all that afternoon getting up the main runners for the first floor, about seven feet off the ground. D.G. figured out a way to make a ramshackle ladder about eight feet high. They leaned the ladder inside the square of trees and nailed one end of a pole to the tree. Linc held the other end as high as he could. Then they moved the ladder to the other side and nailed in the end. It took awhile, but in less than an hour they had all four runners up.

"Now all we have to do is make a floor and we'll have the first platform in," D.G. said as he wiped his forehead.

The woods steamed. It had to be over a hundred degrees. With the additional odors of skunk cabbage and stagnant water drifting up from the lower areas, Everett wondered if they could stand building a whole fort in that atmosphere. He thought it would be great if Linc and Tina's pool had been filled. He could use a good swim.

"We really need flat boards for the flooring, don't we?" Linc asked. His reddish blond hair glinted in the light that streamed through the leafy ceiling over them.

"We could go over to the school," Tina added. "There's a lot of used lumber lying around."

"Hey, what about Seth—maybe he could get some for us," Everett said. "He's working there. I bet Seth could get us a lot of good stuff."

"He's probably there now," D.G. said, scratching his head and wiping his face again. "We could get out of this heat for a while anyway."

"Let's do it," Everett said. "We'll have a whole platform done in a couple days."

They dropped their tools and gathered them into a pile, left them at the site, swung across the creek on the rope swing, and headed up to the school. They found Seth and asked him. He pointed to a pile of cut-up and broken slats, two-by-fours, beams, and other things on the north side of the building.

"Just don't go sticking yourselves with a nail," Seth said. As usual he had on his overalls, but today he was wearing a green JOHN DEERE cap, with a few grease marks on it, definitely broken in nicely. "We'd have to haul you off to the doctor. And I'm sure you wouldn't want that."

Everett's brother, Lance, had a wagon, and Tina and Linc had an old wheelbarrow in their garage, so they went home and picked them up, then brought them back to the site. When they finally loaded them up with a number of boards, it all looked perfect. D.G. commandeered the whole operation. They were ready to roll, both barrow and wagon piled high with their take.

"Linc and Everett—you two pull. Tina will hold Linc's pile and I'll hold Everett's. That way it won't spill."

They slowly wound down the street toward the Wattersons' house. Suddenly Everett stopped. "How are we going to get it across the creek?"

D.G. smiled. "Israeli brains—remember? That shallow spot where you and Tina were yesterday."

As they started again, Tina said, "Do you think we'll all be friends when we grow up?"

"Sure," D.G. said. "Friends are people who stick with each other even when they haven't seen each other for a while. Once a friend, you can never not be a friend even if the years separate you. That's what my grandfather says."

"Yeah, but I mean like this," Tina said.

"I will," D.G. said. "Maybe we should make a pact."

"I thought we already did that," Linc answered.

"Another one," D.G. said. "All right, put your toes in."

Everyone stood together and stuck the tip of a sneaker into a circle.

"Now touch fingertips," D.G. said.

Each of the other three stuck out a right index finger. Their toes and fingers joined, D.G. intoned, "Until earth moves, wind falls off the end of the sea, the sea rolls back into ice, and fire ceases to burn bright, may our friendship never cease."

They were all suddenly silent. Then D.G. beamed. "It's done. The pact can never be broken."

They stood up. "Where did you learn that?" Tina asked as she brushed off her shorts.

"From an old wise man," D.G. said, giving them his mysterious squinty-eyed look.

"What's his name?" Everett said, still rather amazed at D.G.'s eloquence.

"T.S.S.B.O.D.G.F.," D.G. quickly spelled.

"TSOABODAGIF?" Tina said, sounding it out slowly. "Who on earth is that?" She wrinkled her nose and glanced at Everett skeptically.

"The Super Smart Brain of D.G. Frankl," D.G. said. "I made it up."

"You made it up!" Tina said, putting her hands on her hips. "How is that supposed to keep us being friends?"

"Oh, nothing'll ever part you morons!" a voice behind them suddenly said. "Morons of a feather flock together."

Everyone spun around. Chuck and Stuart blustered toward them. "Having fun, children?" Chuck asked with a sarcastic grin on his face.

D.G. whispered, "Let's just keep going like nothing's

happening. We don't want to get involved in an argument."

"What are you whispering about, Frankl? Got a secret we should know about?"

Chuck and Stuart stopped and looked at the wagons. "Stealing stuff from the school again, I see," he said, running his hand along a board.

"We didn't steal anything," D.G. said.

"You sure about that?" Chuck asked. "My gramps says Jews'll steal anything."

Everett noticed D.G.'s birthmark flame and his hands bunch into fists, but then he seemed to relax. D.G. turned to the group. "I think we'll recommend that his mouth be washed out with soap, what do you think?"

"Definitely," Tina said, staring at Chuck through slit eyes.

"You and whose army?" Chuck said menacingly.

Everett set his jaw and placed one of the boards back on the wagon. "Come on, Chuck, we're just getting some timber, that's all. It's a free world."

"For what?"

D.G. stepped forward. "Look, Chuck, we asked permission. They said we could take as much as we want. Do you want to be part of it?"

"Already acting like a lawyer, aren't you, Frankl?" Chuck said. But then his face took on a curious look. "What for?"

"For our new fort," D.G. said. "We're building a huge fort behind Linc and Tina's house."

Chuck snorted. "Baby stuff. You think I want to be part of that?"

Grinning, D.G. said, "Yeah, we are kind of babyish, but it's still fun if you're babies like us."

Everett sensed D.G. was trying his strategy—to humor Chuck out of the attack mood. So he moved closer to Stuart. "We have a stock of Gerber's already, and plenty of milk and bottles. We like to drink."

For a moment, Chuck stared at Everett and D.G., looking from one to the other, then he spat onto the ground. "You people are nuts." He started to move away, but then he said, "My gramps has told me about how Jews are taking over everything. So don't get wise, Frankl. I'll bust you in the face."

"Well, there are those who say it could use some rearranging," D.G. said.

Linc and Tina chuckled behind them and Everett laughed out loud. But Chuck gave them a hard look. "Think it's all real funny, huh? Well, we'll see about that. Just stay out of my woods."

"Oh, you bought it?" D.G. said. This time Everett could see he was angry.

"Yeah, I bought it from the Jews who made it stink."

D.G. instantly gave his armpits a sniff. "Funny, I used my deodorant this morning, too. You smell anything, Tina?"

Immediately, Tina leaned forward and gave D.G. a sniff. "No, must be something else."

"Sorry. We didn't cause the stink," D.G. said, shaking

his head. "But if you want to see our fort sometime, give us a call." He signaled to everyone to get the wagon and wheelbarrow moving. D.G. gave Chuck a curt salute, then turned to the others. "Wagon train, ho-up!"

A moment later, they pulled past Chuck and Stuart. The two boys watched openmouthed as the foursome went by. No one said anything, until they'd gotten about twenty feet down the road. Then Chuck called after them, "What are you really building, Frankl—a synagogue?"

D.G. whipped around. "No, I told you, a fort. But it'll be reversible. When you turn it inside out it's a trof."

"A trough?"

"Not for pigs," D.G. called. "T-R-O-F."

"What's that?" Chuck asked, scratching his head and turning to Stuart, neither of them getting the joke.

"Look it up," D.G. said as they wheeled to the end of the street. "Quiz on Saturday."

Everyone laughed, releasing the tension again, and Tina commented, "Hit him with your best shot."

D.G. chuckled. "That'll keep him busy."

But as they walked on, Everett said, "That was pretty slick, D.G. You told him the truth without telling him the truth. We are building a fort and it will be behind Linc and Tina's house."

"Yeah, I figure that'll throw him off, and if he accuses me of lying I can honestly say I didn't lie about a thing."

No one said much more about the encounter that day. They worked till past four o'clock at the tree fort, then went home for dinner. On the way up the hill, Tina finally said, "D.G., aren't you the least little worried about Chuck finding out about our real tree fort?"

Shrugging, D.G. said, "Yeah, I guess. But what can we do?"

Suddenly there were tears in his eyes. "I hate that stuff. All my life I've heard about how Hitler killed the Jews. How people have hated Jews. My parents thought . . ."

Everyone stood around D.G. Tina put her hand on D.G.'s shoulder. "It's okay. We don't feel that way."

D.G. nodded. "I know. But sometimes . . ." He turned away.

"It's not right," Linc suddenly cried, punching his fist into his hand. "No one should act that way."

Everett was watching D.G. The smaller boy began walking away.

"D.G.!"

He stopped.

They all crowded around him.

"Put your hands in," Everett said suddenly.

Tina, Linc, and Everett stuck their hands into the middle of the circle. D.G. turned around slowly. His face looked beaten, broken.

"Put them in, D.G.," Everett said again.

D.G. slowly put his hands in.

"Repeat after me. We will never desert each other."

The other three repeated it. "We will never desert each other."

"No matter what happens."

"No matter what happens."

"No matter who attacks."

"No matter who attacks."

"We will stand together and never give up."

Everyone said it. Everett looked from eye to eye. Tina's eyes had filled with tears, and Linc's cheek was throbbing. D.G. wouldn't look at anyone.

"By God's power we will stand against all enemies."

Everyone repeated it.

"And by God's power we will win."

Even as Everett said it, he felt strangely strong. When everyone had said it, he concluded, "Amen."

They stood still, their hands still in the middle. No one spoke. D.G. finally looked around at everyone. "Thanks," he said. "I needed that. I guess you made that one up, too."

"Yeah," Everett said and smiled. Tina wiped her eyes.

Then D.G. said, "So am I a Christian now or something?"

They all laughed. With that, they clapped one another on the back and began walking toward their homes.

"It'll work out," Linc called as he reached his driveway. "It will."

Everett felt a surge of confidence. Chuck or no Chuck, they were going to stand together. No one could shake them now.

After they'd all arrived at the tree fort the next morning, Everett brought it right up. "Why do you think Chuck is so against D.G.?"

D.G. pounded a nail out of one of the boards backward, then pulled it. Linc and Tina worked on other boards. Everett had begun braiding a rope ladder at D.G.'s suggestion.

"It's obvious," D.G. said. "Chuck's been influenced by someone who's a real bigot."

Linc looked up from his work. "What on earth is that?"

Tina stood with her hands on her hips. "Ugh, I don't

believe it, Linc! You don't know what a bigot it. It's like the Ku Klux Klan and black people. It's someone who hates someone else of a different group for no good reason."

Linc looked embarrassed, and Everett gave him a sympathetic look. Even though he'd heard the term and even used it, he hadn't been sure what it meant. Linc commented, "Don't have to treat me like an idiot, Tina. It's not like you get straight As or anything."

"Everyone knows what a bigot is."

"Well, I didn't."

"Hey, hey!" D.G. interrupted. "No reason to argue. There's no reason to be upset about this. It's a perennial problem for Jews."

Linc hung his head, but Everett quickly interjected, "Okay, what's peren—what is it?"

D.G. laughed. "Perennial. It means . . ." He got that sly look again. "It's British. Wives used to tell their husbands that was where to put the garbage. 'Put it in any 'ole, Al.' But they said it real fast. Pu-renni-ol."

"Get out of here!" Linc answered with a chuckle.

"D.G.'s cracking jokes again," Tina said. But Everett felt better that at least D.G. could joke about it.

"No, it means it happens regularly or constantly."

"Right," said Tina. "Like perennial flowers grow every year."

Linc scowled at her, and Tina crossed her arms with triumph, but Everett just grinned. He liked the banter. It made him feel like they would never not be friends. Ever.

"Anyway," D.G. said, "to make it short, Jews have always dealt with bigotry so it's no big deal to me."

"It's still not right," Tina said.

"Not much in this world is right," D.G. said and turned back to the tree. Tina grimaced and went back to her work.

Everett worked up his courage to say what he'd been thinking about. "What if Chuck just feels left out? What if we really did invite him to be part of our group? What if we asked him to join the tree fort?"

D.G. stood, wrinkling his eyebrows. Tina turned around and stared at Everett, obviously amazed. Linc worked on a nail. He was the only one who spoke. "Yeah, and in five minutes he'd want to take over. And in five more minutes he'd be pounding one of us because we looked at him wrong."

The forest suddenly seemed quiet and hot. Everett wondered if he'd said the wrong thing. D.G. seemed to be thinking and rubbed his chin. Tina looked from Everett to D.G., obviously a bit confused. "You don't really want him to be part of this, do you? After the things he's done?"

"He is a neighbor," Everett said. "We can't go for the rest of our lives acting like we're mortal enemies."

After a moment of thought, D.G. nodded. "Maybe you do have a point. It's the same thing the Americans always do after a war. Like with the Marshall Plan."

Tina rolled her eyes. "Don't start in with a history lesson, D.G.," she said, giving D.G. a frustrated look.

"Really," D.G. answered. "Americans are always beating

their enemies, then after they've mauled them they rebuild them and make them friends. Look at Germany today. Look at Japan. Look at Italy. Look at Russia!"

"So?" Tina said. "That's countries. All sorts of people are involved. We're just kids."

"It could work the same way," D.G. said. His eyes were suddenly alight with excitement. He appeared to want to do it more than anyone else, even Everett. "But we'd have to test it out first."

Tina shook her head. "I say forget the guy. Let him grow up a little."

Linc grunted approval. But Everett said, "What do you mean, 'Test it out'?"

Dropping his axe, D.G. began to pace. His PENN STATE sweatshirt already clung to his chest and arms. It was hot, and everyone was sweating. The tousle-haired boy said, "We don't want him to know about the tree fort—right? Not unless we're sure we can trust him. So we have to find out if we can trust him. See if he'll really try to get along."

After a moment of looking around at one another, Tina sat down and Linc joined her. Both looked up at D.G. Everett took a seat next to them. D.G. finally settled down opposite them, his back against one of the four trees. "There must be some way to find out," he said. "A game or something."

"My birthday's next week. Remember, July 25?" Everett said. "I had been trying to decide whether to invite him."

D.G. sucked his lip. Tina and Linc were silent. The woods seemed to have gone dead quiet. D.G. said, "Okay, this is the plan. Invite Chuck and Stuart. We'll just play it by ear. I mean, I guess you're going to invite all of us."

"Of course." Everett gave him an amazed look.

"Sorry, just have to make sure we're all thinking together." D.G. tugged at his nose, scratching it. "Bugs all over the place." He wiped his nose on the back of his right hand. "All right. You'll probably have some games and stuff. How many people will be there?"

Everett quickly gave him a list. Besides them, his own family, and Chuck and Stuart, there would be his grandparents from Collingswood and several cousins and friends. "Probably about twenty people or so."

"Good," D.G. said. "Lots of people to mingle with. So we'll all try to be honestly friendly with Chuck and see what happens. I mean 'honestly friendly.' We can't fake it. We really have to try. If in the end Chuck starts anything, it'll be plain he hasn't accepted our peace offering."

"Peace offering?" Tina murmured.

"Oh, now who's the dum-dum?" Linc remarked immediately, raising his eyebrows dramatically.

"So you know what a peace offering is, dufus-head?" Tina turned and punched her brother in the arm.

"Okay, eat a mosquito sandwich," D.G. said. "It's just an expression. Anyway, that's what we'll do. We'll really try to be friends with Chuck. And maybe you could do a little diplomacy with Chuck yourself, Ev."

Tina sighed. "We all have to have three degrees to understand you, D.G."

"You don't know what diplomacy is?"

"Right, and neither does Linc or Everett."

Everett and Linc laughed.

"Man, I'm going to have to do some major major major remedial work with you all," D.G. said with a crinkly grin. Then he sighed and said quietly, "I'm sorry. I'm not trying to show off. . . ."

"We know that," Tina said, banging her foot on the ground. "Just speak English and remember who you're talking to: me, regular B student; Everett, who's smart but not number one; and the complete dufus-brain I have for a brother."

"Hey!" Linc said, but he was smiling.

"Anyway," D.G. said, "diplomacy is the ability to handle tricky affairs between people and nations."

Grinning, Tina added, "And I suppose you just happened to have remembered that definition from *Webster's Dictionary*."

"Oh, look who's talking smart now," Linc said and gave Tina a push.

She groaned and sat up. "All right. I'll go along with this peace offering, I guess. But I think we all know how it will turn out."

"Well, at least we're giving him a chance," D.G. said.

"We may be surprised, too," Everett answered. "You never know. My dad says God can do the impossible."

"If He can straighten out this one, I'll believe anything," D.G. said.

Tina and Linc smiled. Everett nodded his head, thinking, *I'll even pray about it.*

They pulled nails all morning and got half the first platform floored. D.G. suggested bracing each under-runner with a two-by-four. Tina was the first to stand on the finished part of the platform. Then Everett climbed up and joined her. D.G. didn't think they should have more than two at a time on it. He and Linc tried it after Tina and Everett came down. It was looking good.

That afternoon a truck arrived to fill up Tina and Linc's pool. The four of them sat out by the pool and watched it fill up. Then they all went home and put on bathing suits. They still couldn't swim until the filter was in operation and the water was properly chlorinated, but Mr. Watterson had that done by late afternoon. Everyone took a dip, and they sailed around in the little green plastic boats Mr. Watterson had bought. Then they helped him set the diving board in place.

That night Everett decided to make the first attempt at diplomatic relations. He called Chuck. Mrs. Davis answered.

"This is Everett, Mrs. Davis. Is Chuck there?"

"Sure, Everett. I'll get Chuck."

A moment later, Chuck came on. Obviously, Mrs. Davis had told him it was Everett.

"Yeah?"

"This is Everett, Chuck."

"Yeah?"

Everett tried to think of some ways to break the ice, but every avenue led to something Chuck probably didn't want to discuss. Maybe it was best just to be direct.

"You know, my birthday's coming up next week."

"So?"

"Uh, well, I was having a party and . . ."

"What, you just want me to give you a present?"

"No, I thought, maybe . . . I thought, maybe you'd like to come. Like old times."

"Yeah, right."

Real sarcastic, Everett thought forlornly. This was definitely not going to work. But he said, "No, really, Chuck. There's no reason for us to act like we were never friends."

"Oh, were we at one time?"

Everett paused, noticing he was trembling. He stood barefoot in his parents' bedroom. The house was quiet. He hadn't said anything to his mother or father about inviting Chuck.

"Chuck, you live almost across the street. We ought to make an attempt to get along. I thought maybe if you came to the party we could be friends again. Who knows what could happen?"

"I suppose the Jew will be there."

"D.G.?"

"You know any other Jews?"

Everett swallowed. Was he really that prejudiced? "Come on, Chuck. D.G.'s okay. He's not a bad guy. He wants to be friends with you."

"Oh, he does, does he? Like what he wrote in that notebook of his." Chuck referred to a trick Everett, D.G., and the others had played on Chuck earlier that summer.

After pausing, Everett said, "That was a big mistake, Chuck. We're all sorry. That's why we didn't keep it."

"Yeah, well . . ."

"Look, it'll be like old times. We can play croquet, eat some hot dogs and hamburgers; it'll be great. Come on. We can't act like we've never been friends." It was amazing how hard it was. Why was Chuck being so stubborn about it?

"I'll think about it. That's all I can say."

"Stuart's invited, too."

"I'll tell him."

"I hope you'll come. It's next Saturday."

"I said I'll think about it."

"All right."

They both hung up. Everett noticed he was shaking. *Was that how the men felt who tried to get the Arabs to talk to the Jews? How did they stand it?* Suddenly he laughed. *So that's diplomacy? Seems like pussyfooting around to me.*

Everyone that Everett invited came, even Chuck and Stuart. Chuck was wearing a rabbit's foot about his neck, which Everett knew was his "lucky hare." He'd always thought it rather dumb, but Chuck often did things like that.

Seth visited for a little while, then had to go off to work. Whip and Bump, who seemed a bit amazed at all the attention, performed their tricks perfectly. Seth ended up leaving Whip and Bump in the care of Linc and Tina. Everett's cousins were there, too, and his grandparents.

D.G. arrived last. At first, Everett thought D.G. might

not show, but he finally ambled in, his hair combed, and everything about him spic and span. He was dressed in chino slacks and a green tennis shirt. He looked different—and great. He had a large present in his hand and something else in a bag. When he came in the front door, he handed the bag to Everett's mother. Chuck was standing nearby, watching.

"I know you're having hot dogs and hamburgers," D.G. told her. "But I'll have to eat these. I hope you don't mind."

Mrs. Abels looked surprised. "Are you on a diet, D.G.?"

"No, my family's kosher—on Saturdays anyway. Sometimes I'm not supposed to eat certain things. It's a weird rule, but until I'm twenty-one my father says I have to abide by it. Sometimes he lets me overlook it, but he was in his kosher mood last night."

Smiling, Mrs. Abels said, "Oh, that's fine. I'll put it in the refrigerator."

A moment later, D.G. glanced at Everett and beamed. "Here's your present."

"It didn't have to be so big."

"Something we definitely need."

As Everett turned around, he noticed Chuck eyeing D.G., but he said nothing. Everyone else had gathered out back.

"Come on," Everett said. "We're having a badminton contest."

Everyone grouped around the badminton net, watching different pairs play. Linc had paired with a cousin of

Everett's named Billy, and after several games they were undefeated. Even Chuck and Stuart failed to dislodge them. After that there were sack races, one-legged races, a tug-of-war, and other events. Everyone got a prize or two. Everett noticed that D.G. hung back from the crowd a bit, and he figured it was a shyness he hadn't seen before. Even D.G. couldn't do everything.

Chuck on the other hand seemed his old, jovial self. He cracked jokes, flirted with another of Everett's cousins named Pam, and won several races. Everett's hopes soared.

Moments later, Linc whispered to Everett, "It's not going bad," he said. "But Chuck and Stuart are really eyeballing D.G. I think we'd better help D.G. feel more like he fits in. I think he feels a little weird."

Everett said quickly, "Let's go rescue D.G."

A croquet game was beginning. D.G. was still standing on the patio with his hands in his pockets, not really participating. But Everett walked over and asked him to play in the croquet match.

D.G. said, "I never played that game before."

"It's simple," Everett said and explained the rules. D.G. joined him reluctantly, but after a few quick shots through the wickets, he caught the fervor.

Only eight could play, and Chuck decided to join them. Everett breathed more easily. D.G. seemed to be getting the hang of it and nothing bad had happened. Chuck even seemed friendly.

Then suddenly Chuck and D.G. were arguing.

"You took three strokes, Scarface," Chuck said, his face red and angry, the rabbit's foot jumping and bobbing on the chain around his neck.

D.G. flinched when Chuck used the old nickname and shrank into his collar at the sudden attention. Taking his time, D.G. explained what had happened. "I hit Pam. That gave me two strokes. I used them getting through the far right wicket. Then I hit you and got two more strokes. That got me through the middle wicket."

"You took three strokes after hitting me," Chuck countered.

Everett hurried over with Linc. He hadn't seen whether D.G. had taken two or three. But he'd never known D.G. to cheat. Pam, however, said D.G. had only taken two hits. "I was watching. He only took two."

"Well, I was watching, too," Chuck said, "and he took three. His ball goes back." He kicked it in the direction of D.G.'s last hit. D.G. promptly picked it up and placed it where it had finally rested. But as the argument rose, Mrs. Abels hurried across the yard with Everett's grandfather and Mrs. Davis.

"Boys, let's calm down."

"I only took two strokes," D.G. insisted.

Chuck suddenly seethed, "Jews are always cheating. Just like you did at badminton, Scarface. Jews always cheat."

"What?" Everett said. "Nobody cheated at badminton."

"I saw him," Chuck said. "He called some shots out that really weren't."

Mrs. Abels was aghast. So was Chuck's mother. "How could you say something like that, Chuck?" she cried. "I think you owe this boy an apology. You don't come from that kind of family."

"That's what Granddad says," Chuck asserted.

Mrs. Davis blushed. Everyone looked very nervous. She caught her breath though and said, "If you don't apologize this instant, you're going home. Whether the boy cheated or not is not now the point."

Glancing around, Everett knew now that D.G. and Chuck being friends was probably impossible. D.G. waited and everyone seemed on edge. But Chuck suddenly said, "Sorry. I thought you took three shots."

"It could have been a mistake on my part, I don't know," D.G. said quickly, looking directly into Chuck's eyes. The bigger boy didn't return the gaze.

"He only took two," Pam said firmly.

"Okay, forget the number of hits he took," said Mrs. Abels. "D.G., why don't you just go back to where you were before this started and do it again?"

D.G. readily agreed. Chuck looked angry, but then more like a cornered rat than anything else. He clearly had lost even though D.G. was taking the shot over.

As Mrs. Abels and Chuck's mother walked back, Everett heard Mrs. Davis say, "I don't know what is getting into that boy. Seems he can't get along with anyone anymore."

Things were quiet after that. Chuck ended up winning

at croquet and even joking to D.G., "Thought you could beat me, huh, Frankl?"

At being called by a real name, D.G. just shrugged. He said, "You win some, you lose some."

Following the games, Whip and Bump performed for the group. Rollovers. Retrieving several balls. Everett's cousins were enthralled. Then Everett opened his presents. He received a number of great items, including a Phillies cap and a watch from his parents, a game of Monopoly from Linc and Tina, and a Swiss army knife from D.G., which he'd wrapped inside several boxes to make it look a lot bigger than it was. Chuck gave him a tank model and Stuart had picked out a shirt with a surfer on the front.

As lunchtime rolled around, everyone lined up for their respective hot dog or hamburger. Chuck and Stuart leaned against the side of the house, watching as D.G. came to the head of the line. He peered at the charcoal cooker, but the two white-skinned franks he'd brought were gone. "I brought the kosher franks," D.G. said.

Mr. Abels looked at the grill. "They were right here a minute ago, D.G. I don't know what could have happened."

Those close by looked around, and then Everett turned just in time to see Whip and Bump each scarfing down a hot dog. Chuck and Stuart grinned and munched their own hamburgers.

Then Mr. Abels spotted the dogs. "How did those dogs get hold of D.G.'s franks? I was keeping a careful watch."

No one said anything, but Pam, who was turning out to

be the eagle eye of the group, said, "They gave them to the dogs." She pointed to Chuck and Stuart. Chuck instantly feigned innocence, but a sly grin crossed his face.

Mrs. Davis stalked over to Chuck and eyed him. "Did you feed that boy's lunch to those dogs?"

Chuck didn't back down. "We thought they were for them."

"You did not!"

Everyone had turned in their direction. "It was a joke, Mom."

"So you did give the hot dogs to the two Dobermans?"

"Mom, it was a joke. We were only . . ."

"Don't give me that!" Mrs. Davis looked like she was about to smack Chuck right on the cheek. She hovered over him, angry and frustrated.

D.G. said, "It's all right. I'll eat chips and dip and stuff."

Shaking her head, Mrs. Davis seethed, "You owe this boy a big apology this time, young man. First, the way you talked at croquet and now this. This is abominable behavior. Just abominable!" She dragged him by the ear over to D.G. and Mr. Abels. Everyone gaped. "Tell him you're sorry. No quibbling."

Chuck cried, "It was a joke!"

Mrs. Davis squeezed his arm tight. "You're headed for a major grounding. Now tell this boy you're sorry."

For a moment, the big boy hesitated, then he answered, "I'm not saying anything. If he can't take a joke, that's his problem."

"This was no joke." Mrs. Davis turned around, her face red and her hair disheveled. "I'm very sorry about this, Tom, Janet," she said to Everett's parents. "I don't know what's gotten into him." She looked at D.G. "I'm sorry for my son's behavior, and if he won't apologize, I will."

Chuck angrily eyed D.G. who appeared to be trying to disappear into the crowd. Chuck still didn't budge. "I'm not sorry. That stuff was for dogs."

"Are you calling D.G. a dog?" Everett said, now getting angry and feeling defensive about his friend. But his father eyed him and indicated that he should keep his mouth shut.

Chuck looked from his mother to Everett to D.G. "No, I'm just saying I thought it was for the dogs. It looked greasy or something, like what dogs would eat. It was just a joke, for . . . for . . ."

"That's a mighty nasty attitude you have there, Chuck," Mr. Abels said. "You shouldn't be treating people that way."

"Yeah," one of Everett's cousins said. "He's been pushing everybody around in the games, too."

Suddenly, the place erupted, with all the kids saying something negative about Chuck's behavior. For the first time his proud face clouded. He turned, dropped his hamburger on the picnic table, and stomped toward the gate. His mother apologized to everyone, but was right behind him pushing him on the back. Chuck didn't turn around.

Tina stood next to D.G., her face white with fear and

anger. D.G. suddenly said, "It's all right, Mr. Abels. I'm not that hungry anyway."

Patting D.G. on the back, Everett's father said, "Son, you have a good attitude, but we don't want you to be hungry."

To Everett, D.G. suddenly looked small and vulnerable. He obviously did not like being a center of attention. Everett tried to think of something to say, but his mother took control of the situation. "All right, everyone, please sit down. This has been a little harrowing, but please, let's all just eat." She asked her husband to offer a word of prayer, and after that, everyone sat down.

The food, though, tasted like dirt in Everett's mouth. It was wrong. That's all it was. Wrong. Dead wrong. People shouldn't be that way. But plainly, that was exactly the way it was.

That evening, when everyone was gone, Everett sat miserably at the dinner table having some ice cream and cake with his family. They ate silently, spoons and forks clinking on the plates. Finally, Everett's mother sighed. "I'm sorry, honey. I hope you don't feel like it was a ruined day."

"I don't."

Everett's brother, Lance, not quite sure what had happened, piped up, "D.G. should have punched Chuck right in the nose."

"Now, Lance," Mr. Abels said.

But Jillie answered, "It was a mean thing to do."

Everett stared into his melting vanilla ice cream. "Why is he that way, Dad? What did I do wrong?"

Mr. Abels shook his head. "The sins of the fathers. . ." he said mysteriously.

Looking at his father, Everett waited expectantly. Mr. Abels sighed and his mother glanced at him nervously. "You should know, Everett, that Chuck's grandfather is a very prejudiced man. I know Chuck's mom and dad have tried hard to avoid it, but Chuck's grandfather is a real firebrand. Someone told me—I don't know for certain that it's true—that he was from the old south and had connections to some rather violent organizations."

"Like the Ku Klux Klan?" Everett asked quickly, remembering how he'd seen some things on TV about them.

"Like that." Mr. Abels cleared his throat. "I've talked to Jim now and then about it, and I know he's very ashamed of it. But he doesn't feel he can stop his own father from seeing his grandson. Chuck's grandfather believes that Jews are the financiers of the world and that they control governments, politicians, and whole industries. It's an old rumor—not true—but plenty of people believe it. I guess Chuck has been deeply influenced."

"But the Davises were always such nice people. They were always having parties for the Little League and everything." Everett raised his eyes to look at his father and waited. Mrs. Abels appeared very uncomfortable.

Then she said quietly, "Everyone has their secrets, Evvie. Everyone. You rarely know a person well unless you live with them. Believe me, it was quite a shock to us when we found out about it."

Everett took another bite of cake. Suddenly he felt very sick inside. "But D.G.'s such a nice guy."

Mr. Abels shook his head. "Being a nice guy has nothing to do with it. Prejudice only sees what it wants to see. And when Chuck looks at D.G., he doesn't see nice kid, smart guy, loyal, or friendly, he sees Jew, and that means someone to hate regardless of what he's like as a person."

"But that's wrong, Dad. That's wrong."

"Sure it is. But saying it's wrong won't change it because people like that think they're right and everyone else is wrong."

"But how can that be?" Everett clenched his fist. "It's not fair."

Mr. Abels sighed. "Ev, it's like this. Everyone has things about them that others don't like. God didn't make us all the same. But God did give us laws to help us all learn to get along. Unfortunately, plenty of people don't feel they have to abide by those laws. They could care less what God, the government, or anyone else says.

"So the question is, what do you do about people who hate others without cause? And the answer is, not much. You can pray for them. You can argue with them and confront them. But in the end, unless they're doing something criminal, there's not a whole lot you can do to stop them."

"But it is criminal, Dad. What Chuck did to D.G. was awful."

"Criminal in the sense that it breaks the laws of the land, Ev. That's what I mean by criminal. And sure, it was criminal—from a certain perspective. But ultimately, Chuck's parents have to deal with it, and in the end Chuck has a right to have his own beliefs, even at his age."

"But, Dad, it's . . ."

"Unfair?"

"Yeah. Really unfair."

"All of life is unfair, Ev. There's no justice in this world. We'll have to wait for the next one to get that."

Everett chewed his lip with frustration. Lance and Jillie looked back and forth between him and his father. His mother gazed at him sympathetically. She reached across the table and took his hand. "You're growing up, honey. It's not a bed of roses out there. Bad things happen."

"But we should do something about it, Mom."

"Like what?" His mother fixed him with her gray eyes that were at once solid and strong and also warm and embracing. Everett always felt loved when she looked at him that way.

"If you've talked to Chuck, if you've tried to make peace, if you've really worked at settling the differences, and he doesn't want any of it, what can you do?"

"Defend yourself," Everett said sullenly.

Mr. Abels nodded. "Yes, that may be what it comes down to."

Everett looked away. His ice cream had melted. The chocolate cake was soggy. He felt as though the whole world was nuts. "Yeah, and then they come at you with bullets," Everett murmured.

His dad's eyes were still on him. "What's that, Ev?"

"Nothing. Just thinking, that's all."

His mother let go of his hand. She said, "That's what a family's for, honey. To help you work through these things. I'm glad you told us."

"Doesn't do much good," Everett said.

She smiled. "It does more good than you know."

11 A Way to Make Peace

Everett didn't see the group the next day because of church in the morning and a visit to a great-aunt that afternoon. But on Monday, they all had a chance to discuss the party. It ended with D.G.'s comment, "Well, now I guess we know where we stand. But I don't think we should jump to conclusions. It's always possible things will change."

"What do you think he'll do?" Tina asked angrily. "I can't believe anyone can act like that and get away with it."

"Anything's possible," Everett said. "Chuck's the kind

of guy who holds grudges. Long ones. Real long ones. He wants to hurt you, too. I know."

Tina gazed at D.G. sympathetically. Linc was all for going over to Chuck's house and pounding him one. D.G. answered, "I think the best thing to do is to talk to Seth."

"Seth?" Everyone said together.

"He's very wise and maybe he'll have an idea we haven't hit on," D.G. answered, looking at them with astonishment. "Don't you think Seth can help?"

"Sure," Tina replied. "But . . . well, yeah, maybe we should go to Seth." She glanced at the others and everyone quickly agreed.

"That's what I thought," D.G. said. "So let's go up this afternoon when he gets home from work."

They worked on the tree fort, then headed up to Seth's after three-thirty when he usually got home. When D.G. finished explaining what had happened, he folded his arms and said, "And we don't know what to do."

They sat around Seth's table sipping iced tea. Whip's head lay on Tina's lap as she stroked his ears. Bump rested at Everett's feet. The cabin was cool inside, even without air-conditioning, and it felt good to be in the safety of the cabin.

After sitting back and taking a long slug of iced tea, Seth said, "When in trouble, always turn to the Good Book."

"The Bible?" D.G. answered skeptically.

"Sure enough," Seth said, picking his Bible up off an

end table and flipping it open. It was a thick, black, leather-covered book with lots of writing on the margins. It looked as if it might fall apart any moment. "There were plenty of people in the Bible who had real problems with other folks, sometimes to the point that their enemies wanted to kill them. Like David and King Saul."

"Oh, right," D.G. said. "David's the greatest king of Israel."

"But before he was king," Seth answered, "he had lots of trouble with Saul who was God's first chosen king."

Everett said, "King Saul was jealous because the people liked David more than him and even said he'd done more."

"Exactly," Seth said. He began to read in the Book of I Samuel about how the people chanted: "Saul has slain his thousands and David his ten thousands." Then Seth explained, "God had rejected Saul because he was rebellious. He raised up David and made him more important. Saul wanted to kill him. Then God sent an evil spirit to make Saul's life miserable. He was one unhappy redneck."

D.G. laughed, but Seth only said, "Just an expression. But the interesting thing is that David had one big chance to do Saul in."

"When he tore off a piece of the king's robe," D.G. said, glancing around at the others. When everyone stared at him with awe, he said, "Hebrew school, every Saturday. Rabbi's favorite story."

"David and his men was hidin' in a cave," Seth said.

"And Saul went in to relieve himself, then fell asleep. All his men was whisperin' that now was David's chance to kill off the bum once and for all. But David told them he couldn't touch God's anointed and that was that. But he did sneak up and cut off a sliver of Saul's robe. Later, when Saul was back with his men, David went out and showed him, to prove he meant him no harm."

"But it didn't do any good," Everett said sadly.

"No, it didn't," Seth said. "But it did a lot of good for David."

Tina sat up straight suddenly. "I know—it helped David become more patient and understanding of others."

"That's part of it, Tina," Seth said. "But even more, it showed David was willin' to obey God even if it seemed stupid, or hurtful, to him. That's the big thing about knowing God—obeying Him even when you think it might not help you."

"There was also King David and his son Absalom," D.G. said, fidgeting a little, but still obviously interested.

"Another sad story," Seth said. "And there's Cain and Abel, which ended in a murder, and even Adam and Eve."

"You believe in Adam and Eve?" D.G. asked, his eyes wide.

"Sure enough," Seth said with a little twinkle in his eyes. "None of this evolution stuff for me. But that's not the point. There are plenty of people who couldn't get along. But then there are those who worked out their problems."

"Like who?" D.G. asked.

"Paul and John Mark," Seth said. He flipped over many pages and found a passage in Acts, then another in Timothy. In the first, Paul refused to let John Mark go with him and Barnabas on a journey because the younger man deserted them the first time. But later, Paul asked Timothy to visit with John Mark because the younger man was now "useful to me for service."

"So Paul and John Mark made up," Tina said.

"We don't know what happened," Seth answered. "But they did something. There's also Joseph and his brothers."

"Oh, I know that one," D.G. said. "Where the ten brothers sold Joseph as a slave and then he became Pharaoh's top man and saved them all later."

"And he forgave them all, too," Seth said.

"But the brothers really didn't believe it," D.G. protested.

Seth shook his head sadly. "Sometimes when people forgive others who have hurt them, the ones who did the hurtin' can't take it."

"Maybe that's what we have to do with Chuck," Everett suddenly said. Bump stood up and yawned into his face and everyone laughed. "Looks like Bump is kind of bored with this conversation," Everett said and everyone chuckled again.

"He only likes my dog stories," Seth said with a smile.

There was a long pause as everyone dug into a bag of pretzels Seth produced. Then he said, "Of course, there's one story you all are missin', the greatest makin'-peace story of all."

They all looked up. Then Everett said quietly, "Jesus?"

Seth nodded. "When Jesus died on that cross, He was makin' peace between God and all people the world over."

D.G. looked a bit uncomfortable, and he said, "Jews don't believe in Jesus."

"I understand that, D.G.," Seth said, "and you're free to believe what you want. But that's what Jesus said He came to do. See, God was angry with us because of our sin. Some are killin' others. Some are lyin' and hatin', some are stealin', but they're all doin' something that God says is wrong."

Everyone was silent.

"But God didn't want to leave it that way," Seth went on. "He had to fix things. So He had two big problems. One was dealin' with sin. See, God is so perfect that He can't even stand the sight of that stuff. He had to fix it so people could live with Him after they died. The other problem was changing people so they didn't want to sin anymore. So Jesus did it all in one shot!" Seth clapped his hands and everyone jumped.

Everett gazed at Seth. This was something he had never understood very well, and he listened intently. He noticed even D.G. looked intrigued.

"See, when Jesus died on the cross," Seth said, "God put all our sins on Him. Just smack on. And then He punished Jesus for us so He could let us all off the hook. Jesus took the sin and the rap and now God looks at us like we're no longer sinners."

After taking another long sip, D.G. said, "That's why Christians say Jesus was perfect."

"Right!" Seth said with a grin. "Smart kid!"

"Doesn't mean I believe it," D.G. said with a smile.

"Just so you listen," Seth said. "But see, when Jesus rose from the dead after the cross, then He sent His Spirit to change us on the inside. So God had Jesus pay for our sins, and Jesus sent us the Spirit so we would change."

"But people don't act like it," D.G. said suddenly.

"Yeah, like Chuck," Tina said.

"But like everyone else, too," Linc answered. "The whole world acts mean and nasty to people, too."

"That's the kicker," Seth said. "It doesn't happen to anyone 'less they believe."

"Faith," Everett said. "That's what I did."

Everyone turned to him, and suddenly he felt embarrassed. But then he explained, "Last year in church I decided to believe in Jesus."

"You never told me that," D.G. said, jabbing him in the ribs.

"Haven't told you a lot of things," Everett answered, and they all laughed.

"That's it," Seth said. "You can only make peace with God if you choose to believe in His Son. That's how He did it."

"Jews don't believe that," D.G. protested again.

"I understand that," Seth said kindly. "But some Jews do. And Jesus and His disciples were all Jews, too."

Rubbing his chin, D.G. said, "I never thought of it that way."

"Now let's not get our ball lost in the weeds here," Seth said. "The important thing is that Jesus made peace not by war, but by dying on the cross. Sometimes peace only happens when someone decides to sacrifice hisself."

"Doesn't happen very much like that," D.G. commented.

"But what kind of sacrifice could we make?" Everett asked. "Chuck would laugh in our faces."

"That's the mystery," Seth said, taking a final slug of iced tea. "If you pray about it, God'll show you the way, guaranteed!"

Everyone drank quietly, and then Tina said, "Can you tell us a story, Seth?"

"After all this talk?"

"Yeah!" D.G. exclaimed and everyone else answered, hunkering down in their seats ready for one of Seth's barnstormers.

"OK," Seth said, "I'll tell you 'bout Jesus and the storm. How He made peace by shutting it off just like water out of a spigot." Seth launched into one of his rip-roarers that kept them all entranced for the next fifteen minutes. When it was over, he said it was time for them to get home to dinner. Everett thought about Jesus' sacrifice on the way home, but he saw no way anyone could do something like that. When they finally reached the rope swing, he prayed, "Lord, just help me see what to do."

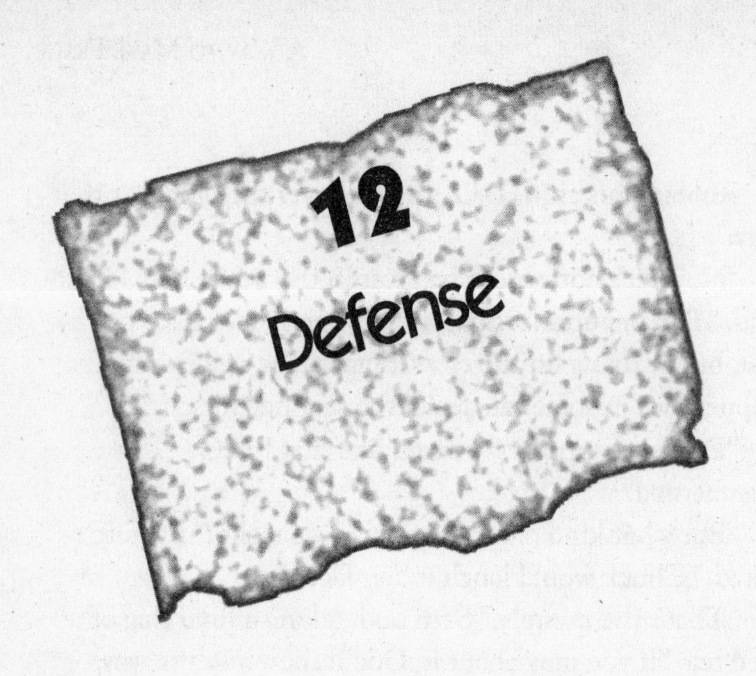

12 Defense

The next afternoon, they all sat on the ground underneath the tree fort, discussing Seth's idea about Jesus and peace. Everyone agreed it was an interesting way to solve a problem, but no one saw how it could happen. In the end, D.G. said, "Let's just sit tight, and maybe Chuck will move or something."

"I don't think that will happen," Tina said.

"Well, maybe there will be a storm," D.G. said, opening his eyes and mouth with fake wonder, "and he'll blow out to the Atlantic."

They caught the mood and soon everyone was joking

about what might happen, but finally Everett said, "Somehow it has to work out."

D.G. looked down at the ground. "Maybe we should just give him the woods and forget the tree fort."

"No!" all three of them answered. "We have a right to be here."

D.G. looked up and into each of their eyes. "Then we have to be ready," he said. "We can't just sit here and let it happen."

Everett didn't know what D.G. meant by that, but he figured they had nothing to lose by preparing for the worst. They spent several afternoons lolling in the Wattersons' pool after a hard morning's work at the tree fort. They played Moby Dick and had numerous sea battles that D.G. said were just like the sinking of the Spanish Armada, the Battle of Salamis with the Greeks and Persians, and the Battle of Midway in World War II. It turned out to be marvelous history for about two minutes, then an all-out crazy splash and clash in the pool.

In another week they had the two floors up at the tree fort. By the time they were done, it was August. There had been no contact with Chuck. The rope ladder now hung down over the edge of the tree fort about seven feet. D.G. rigged up a way to hoist the ladder up so that no could get into the fort when they weren't there. He used pulleys he said he found in his garage. Then he stretched the pull rope down the other side of the tree fort. Tina colored the rope a light gray, so that it was almost invisible unless you were looking directly at it. They had no end of ideas and ways of doing things.

Everett's mother questioned him several times about what they were doing in the woods. He told her, and thought she and his dad might come down to see it. One afternoon he brought up the issue at their council of war, as D.G. called it. They all sat clad in blue jeans shorts and T-shirts on the second floor of the tree fort.

"Maybe we could have a dedication and bring our parents down to see the tree fort," Everett said, hoping no one would be against it.

D.G. replied immediately, "We don't let anyone know about this. It's our fort and parents aren't allowed in."

"But I think it would be cool to show our parents what we've done," Tina said, joining Everett's side. "They might be impressed."

Shaking his head fervently, D.G. said again, "We're not in the business of impressing people. We're here to reclaim the land for the people."

Everett had never seen D.G. so determined. He was sure something else was behind it. But D.G. could be so secretive. No one had ever met anyone else in his family except his mother the few times they'd played in D.G.'s room.

As they sat and talked, D.G. brought up the subject of defense. "How are we going to secure the fort for when we're absent from the premises?"

Linc answered, "Please speaka da English."

D.G. was serious. "Anyone could destroy it if none of us are here. We have to secure it. We have to keep anyone from coming in and trying something."

Screwing up his face, Everett said, "Maybe we ought to invite the Jersey Buckwolf to play bouncer or something." Linc and Tina laughed, but D.G. said they had to be "sober minded about this."

"What we have to do is booby-trap the fort," he said thoughtfully. "Make some things to warn people off. Scare them."

"You mean some signs?" asked Everett.

"Maybe," said D.G. "We'll have to study it. But I don't want Chuck happening upon this place when we're gone. He may just decide to wreck it."

"What can we do?" asked Tina.

"I think we need to plan a defense while we're here. Then we can try to figure out some things to do that might prevent disaster when we're not here."

"Maybe we can make spears and stuff like that," said Everett.

"Good idea," said D.G. "But first we need to work on our slingshot capability. That's probably our best long-range weapon. And we shouldn't make weapons that can really hurt someone. I mean, we are kids."

They all chuckled at that.

"We'll have to have daily practice," D.G. went on. "And we'll have to learn to use several different types of missiles to use in the slings."

"Not just stones and dirt bombs?" asked Everett.

"Sure. But you can't use stones on kids like Chuck and Stuart in a normal situation. We don't want to maim them, just scare them away. We need to think of some things that could be slung at someone without hurting them."

Linc groaned.

"What's the matter?" asked D.G.

He shoved his hand in his pocket. It was bulging. He pulled out a handful of stones. "I thought we might need some."

Grinning, D.G. said, "Good idea. None of us should ever be without our slings and stones. Even if we're not out to hurt anyone." He paused and looked around. "But we need to use things that are less lethal."

"How about little water balloons?" said Everett.

D.G.'s eyebrows went up. "Great idea. Except, what if we used something more frightening than balloons and easier to break?"

"What?" asked Tina.

"Eggs," said D.G., smiling craftily. "Each day we bring down a cache of eggs, maybe one or two apiece. They'll keep for a few days without rotting. Anyone who gets hit with a rotten egg, though, will really regret coming here."

Everett glanced furtively at Linc and Tina. This was definitely fun.

"Now, water balloons," said D.G. "We can throw them, but slinging them may even be better. But what if we fill them with dyed water instead of just plain water, so it makes a big blotch when it hits. Now what else?"

"You know those empty plastic eggs you get at Easter time," said Tina. "I bet we could put something in them that will explode when they hit, too."

"Ooh, how about some vinegar?" said Linc. "That smells awful."

"Excellent," said D.G. "Our enemies will flee before our faces. What else?"

Everett thought of a number of things, from steel balls to firecrackers. "Firecrackers!" he exclaimed.

"Illegal," said D.G. "And someone could really get hurt."

"It might burn down the whole woods, too," said Tina.

"Okay," Everett was thinking fast. "But what about those things at parties that explode. We could rig up some trip lines so that if anyone stepped on them they'd pop. It could be scary if it's happening while everything else is going on."

"Fantastic," said D.G. "And what about this: we string a net up in the tree with four stones at the four corners to weight it down. If someone comes in we can rig it so that we pull a string and the net falls on him."

"Yeah, and how about if when the net falls, something also falls with it—something gooey—like mud," Linc said.

D.G. said, "This is getting to be a major defense session. I've got something else. See that swampy area down there?" He pointed to a marshy area not far from the tree fort. It was the source of some of the numerous mosquitoes that attacked at night. "Those mosquitoes may be our best defense for when we're not here. What if we dig a trench and make a pit filled with marshy gook? Then we cover it. Anyone who steps on it sinks into two feet of mush."

Everett and everyone else were laughing. They didn't notice that three boys had just walked into their site.

Chuck's voice rang out. "Hey, if it isn't Scarface the Jew and his little flock. Hey, Scarface!"

13
The Visit

D.G. shot up and fixed his eyes immediately on Chuck. Everyone scrambled to their feet. Everett dropped down to the first floor through the hole in the second and retrieved his slingshot. On the ground in seconds, D.G. straddled a log in front of the tree fort. Everett followed. "What do you want, Chuck?" D.G. said, his birthmark flaming like a matador's cape.

"To make a lamp shade out of your butt," Chuck said, flicking cigarette ash onto the ground. He sucked at the cigarette, then threw it, still lit, onto some leaves. Everett's heart hammered and he felt sick. Why was Chuck here now?

A light breeze riffled the treetops above them. Stuart stood by Chuck looking wiry and confident. A third boy shifted on the balls of his feet next to Stuart. Everett remembered him from another class at school. He had red hair and freckles and was almost D.G.'s size, though a bit fat. All three of the boys wore blue sweatshirts with "Aces" written on them in black.

"Who do you think you are, building a tree house in these woods?" called Chuck. "These are our woods."

Anger gripped Everett's stomach, but D.G. simply said, "Right, and I suppose Tina's pool is your pool and the United States government is . . ."

"Don't go sassing me," Chuck answered. "I'll bust you quick, Scarface." The other two boys laughed, but Everett suspected the red-haired kid wasn't up to a real fight as Chuck and Stuart might be.

Still, D.G. had no weapons, and Everett realized he didn't have any ammunition for his slingshot. He glanced about seeking something to use. Several acorns lay on the ground, and he bent down to pick them up. Looking up, he noticed the cigarette butt still smoldering where it lay. When no one said anything more, D.G. advanced toward Chuck. "The least you could do is stamp out your cigarette," he said.

"Oh, so now you're Smokey Bear," said Chuck. "You stamp it out."

D.G. hesitated, then walked over to it and ground it in the dirt. He was only a few feet from the bigger boy now.

Everett held back, and he wished D.G. would hustle back to the tree fort where it was safer. But D.G. just stood there.

"Chuck, why can't we just get along?" D.G. suddenly said. "You could build your own tree fort down here if . . ."

"Don't want a tree fort," Chuck said, and spat on the ground in front of D.G.

After a moment's hesitation, Everett hurried over to D.G. He thought maybe he could yank him back to safety.

"Look," D.G. said with a shrug, "you want to make a deal, let's make a deal. We don't have to be nasty to each . . ."

"I'll be any way I want with you. Got it, Frankl?"

Glancing at Everett, D.G. stepped back and took a deep breath. Chuck's two friends stepped forward as Chuck leaned closer to D.G. "What are you going to do, Jew boy, just walk away?" He stepped directly in front of D.G.

D.G. answered, "No. Maybe it would be better just for you to go. Right now, this is our area. You can have any place in the woods you want."

Snorting, Chuck turned to his two friends. "Hear that? We can have any place we want." He leaned forward, his head bobbing about six inches above D.G.'s uncombed brown hair. "Well, what if I want *this* place?"

D.G. stood firm. His birthmark raged through crimson and scarlet and purple. Then Everett moved, and Chuck gave D.G. a shove. D.G. put his arm up to protect himself. "Hey, you have no right to do that," he cried. "There's plenty of woods for everyone."

"Yeah, well maybe I want this part of the woods. What

do you think of that, Scarface?" Chuck slapped the side of D.G.'s head with his hand.

Everett yelled, "Lay off, Chuck. Get out of here."

Putting up his hands, D.G. shouted, "Come on, there's no reason to fight."

"Oh, yeah?" Chuck looked from Everett to D.G., still clipping D.G. on the scalp. "I thought you were going to take me on personally."

Behind them, Linc yelled something at them from in the tree fort, but Everett couldn't hear. His brain seemed fuzzed over. Why didn't D.G. get back under the tree fort? Why was he standing out there taking it?

Then suddenly D.G. put down his hands. "I think we can settle this without fighting."

Chuck's jab flashed like lightning. He clouted D.G. in the face and the smaller boy went down, clutching his nose. Blood oozed out between his fingers.

Immediately, Everett leapt at Chuck. The bigger boy fell back, and Stuart and their red-haired sidekick jumped into the fray. Everett tried to get a punch at Chuck's chin, but missed. A moment later, someone kicked Everett in the stomach. He crumpled over, then Chuck hit him again with an uppercut in the chest. The wind rapped out of him like an explosion. He reached inside himself for air. But he couldn't draw. He fell over, clutching his chest.

Chuck stood over him. "Get up, wimp! Get up and fight."

D.G.'s fingers dripped with blood. Everett felt weak and

dizzy. He tried to rise. Chuck laughed. "Some heroes. Some tough heroes."

Looking at the redness of D.G.'s blood and momentarily forgetting where he was, Everett's heart pounded so loud, he couldn't think. D.G. kept saying, "I'll be all right in a minute; just give me a minute."

Then Chuck suddenly jumped back and looked up, away from D.G. Everett pushed himself into sitting position.

Stones ricocheted into the trees and resounded through the quiet. Two stones dropped beyond them with a thunk. A second later, two more stones rattled into the trees. Linc and Tina were slinging stones over their heads.

D.G. sat up now, watching, holding his nose. Everett got his breath.

Whirling the slings over their heads, Tina and Linc stood firm, each of them on a floor of the tree fort. "Get out of here, Chuck, or the next stone's coming at your nose," shouted Linc. "Believe me, they're hard."

Chuck stared at Linc and gestured. "Fight like a man, jelly belly."

Two more stones whizzed over Chuck's head. He ducked. But Everett could tell the slinging was true. "Get out of here," shouted Tina. Her face was contorted and dark, her eyes black with anger.

As Chuck backed away, Stuart grabbed his arm and said, "Let's leave these sissies. They need a girl to fight for them."

Another stone clattered into the trees only feet over

Chuck's head. Everett looked on in amazement. How had Linc and Tina gotten so accurate? Chuck laughed sarcastically, but turned to go with his two friends.

"We'll be back, believe me," he said. "And next time there won't be no girl in the treetop to save you turkeys." He snorted contemptuously at them all.

Everett swallowed and tried not to move. Then another stone knocked into the trees closer to their heads and the three boys hightailed it. They broke into a run as a spray of stones clattered against tree trunks.

In a few minutes, the woods were silent.

Holding his chest, Everett worked at breathing evenly. He touched D.G. on the shoulder as he lay back on the ground, his fist under his nose. "You okay?"

D.G. nodded. Blood dripped between his fingers. His face was white. But he seemed to know how to stop a nosebleed. "I'll probably have to put it on ice tonight," he said bravely, bending his neck back. "I get these all the time."

Linc and Tina climbed down out of the fort and ran over.

"I can't believe that guy!" yelled Linc. "He thinks he owns the world."

"Are you all right?" Tina asked, stooping down. "It's a good thing . . ."

D.G. took his hand away from his nose and a clump of blood dropped out.

Immediately, Tina ran back to the knapsack. She found

some napkins in the paper bag D.G. stored the cupcakes in, then handed them to D.G. "Maybe this'll help the bleeding."

He stuffed one napkin into his right nostril. He used the other to wipe some of the blood away. "He's real friendly," D.G. said.

Everyone turned and looked in the direction Chuck had gone. Everett's chest still hurt. No question about it, they were out for blood now. He watched Tina as she helped D.G. A strange, icy fear blew over him. All he could see was Chuck pounding his face, kicking him and pounding. A moment later, he was on his feet. A fury burned through him like prairie fire. Suddenly he hated the way Chuck was acting, hated what he believed, hated everything about it. He found a large stone on the ground and hurled it into the trees. "Those creeps! I hate them. I hate them." The stone ricocheted on a branch and thudded to the ground.

Tina, Linc, and D.G. gazed at him in amazement.

"Chuck has no right," Everett yelled. "It's wrong. They have no right to do this to us. There's no way they're taking the tree fort. He can't have it. I don't care what they say. I don't care what they do to us. He has no right. We built the tree fort. They're not driving us away."

Seconds later, his eyes burned with tears. He didn't even know why he was so upset. The sobs crashed through him. It was all going wrong. They were trying to destroy it. He couldn't do a thing about it. No matter how much he tried, they weren't going to let up. That was the way it was in the world. Dog eat dog. Might makes right. The biggest and toughest takes all.

Then it was over.

Everett stopped and rubbed his eyes. The fury vanished. He just felt weak, wrung out. D.G. put his hand on his shoulder. "Hey, it's all right. Nobody's taking the tree fort. Remember what Seth said?"

Staring at him, Everett waited.

"God'll do something incredible, right? Isn't that what Seth said?" D.G. looked from Everett to the others.

"You really believe He will?" Everett said, not even sure D.G. was serious.

"I don't know," D.G. said. "But what else have we got? Everything depends on God in the end, even if we do all we can."

The bloody napkin was still dangling from D.G.'s nostril. Everett stared at it. D.G. looked like some kind of monster they had in one of those rides at Disney World. He could almost feel the thing slithering around.

Everett laughed.

Linc and Tina turned to D.G. They chuckled, too, and pointed at the napkin.

D.G. grinned. "Hey, it's all right. We're all alive." He pulled the napkin out. There was no more bleeding. "That's all there was to it. A little blood and it's over."

He turned to Tina and Linc. "You guys were great. Like William Tell or somebody with that slingshot. How did you do it?"

"We've been practicing," Tina said, her mouth crinkling into a smile.

D.G. laughed. "See, I told you."

"It really works," Tina enthused. "It's a great weapon. I think Linc—he's a better shot—could have put one between Chuck's eyes."

"It's just a good thing I had that pocketful of stones," Linc said sheepishly.

"Yeah, well maybe next time we'll be prepared."

Everett stood up. "At least we didn't chicken and run."

Nodding, D.G.'s eyes glittered with determination. "We have a right to be proud. We didn't buckle under and play dead. We did it. Maybe God—if He's really there—is doing something." There was a pause, then he whooped. "Ai-eeeee!"

Moments later, they were all whooping. Something inside Everett felt stronger now, and secure. Maybe it would be all right. Maybe they could defeat him. And maybe God was doing something. Strange that D.G. would be the one to strengthen that belief.

D.G. went to the knapsack and pulled out the bag of cupcakes. He held them up. "Come on, let's celebrate." He climbed the ladder to the first floor. Everyone followed. D.G. divided up the krimpets. As they ate, D.G. said, "I should have known Chuck'd come. He's sly. We'll just have to be more careful next time. He won't be easy to deal with, but somehow we'll find a way."

Linc flexed his fist. "Maybe we could take him if we

work on it. Maybe if we all lift weights or something."

D.G. shook his head. "Everything in the world doesn't get solved by lifting weights, Linc. No, fistfighting is what he wants. What will defeat him is something else, maybe something about him, some weakness." D.G. paused, then went on. "I don't know what it is. But we'll have to find it. It's got to be brain against brawn. Like the Israelis in the Six-Day War. They outsmarted the Arabs, even when they were totally outnumbered."

Tina said, "Yeah, but what can we do? He's bigger than us."

"First of all," D.G. continued as he stood up on the platform, "we start those defensive measures we talked about. If only we could really scare him—scare him by showing him how wrong he is. That's the best way."

"That's just it," said Linc. "How can we do that?"

"I don't know," D.G. said again. "You can't fight hate with hate. It only makes them stronger. But Seth's idea about love and all, I don't know about that either."

Everett wondered: What would Jesus do? But figuring out how Jesus might handle this was completely beyond him. Sometimes in church everything sounded so easy. But then when you faced it in real life, it never looked that simple. Still, he decided to give Seth's idea a try. And a prayer.

14 Something Different

That night at dinner, Everett had a lot of explaining to do. His cheek was badly bruised and he limped. He told his parents what he could. His father became angry immediately. "I'm calling up Jim Davis and give him a piece of my mind I've should've given him awhile ago."

Everett's mother placed her hand on the phone as he stood to dial. "Before we go rearranging the neighborhood, let's think about this, honey."

"This has gone too far already. It's like we're dealing with Nazis here. I thought that's what World War II was about."

"This isn't World War II." Mrs. Abels stood between him and the phone. Everett sat at the table feeling frustrated. It was nice that his father wanted to do something, but the wrong thing would only make the situation worse.

Shaking his head, Everett's father sat down. His mother sat between them. "Let's pray first."

Instantly, Everett remembered his thought that afternoon, but suddenly it seemed like a useless thing to do. "Mom, everything doesn't get fixed by a prayer."

His mother gazed at him firmly with her gray, see-into-you eyes. She said again, "I know how you all adore action, but sometimes there's a time to sit and wait on the Lord. This is such a time, and I know you know it in your heart."

Everett knew she was right, but sometimes it helped just to hear it from someone who believed it as strongly as she did. His mother prayed, "Please, Lord, help us see our way clear on this. Amen."

When she finished so quickly, Everett felt better. But then his father said, "I just don't see how it could have gotten like this. Chuck always seemed like a fairly normal kid."

Mrs. Abels sighed. "Chuck's mom told me about some of the things Jim's father teaches that boy, and I have to sympathize. The grandfather's a major bigot, Tom. That's all there is to it. And Chuck's going in the same direction."

Everett looked at his glass of Coke, feeling not the least thirsty.

"Anyway, Scripture says we're to love our enemies. So it seems to me . . ."

Sighing, Everett said, "I know that, Mom, but how? I invited him to the party. I talked to him. It's not even me he's that mad at. He just hates D.G. For no reason. Are D.G. and me supposed to hug and kiss him because he beat us up?"

"D.G. and I, honey." His mother patted his hand.

"What?"

"Your English. D.G. and *I*."

"Mom!"

"Don't 'Mom' me. You know how to use proper English."

His father retorted, "Good grief. We've got Adolf Hitler, Jr., for a neighbor, and you're worried about Everett's English."

She laughed and swung back her blonde hair and turned to Everett. "Jesus loved His enemies by dying on the cross for them. That's how God showed He loved us, by dying for us."

It was the same thing Seth had said, Everett remembered. But he asked, "Then what happens—D.G. or me dies for Chuck and his warriors?"

"Of course not," his mother said. "But there are ways. Sometimes kindness, love, and understanding do a lot. Are those things you've tried?"

"We invited him to the party. We haven't antagonized him. We even invited him to build his own tree fort."

"What about asking him to be part of yours?"

Deep down, Everett had known this was coming. He thought about it again. "What if he said yes, then came in and really messed us all up?"

"Do you think he would do that?"

Sighing, Everett said, "I don't know. But the party was the thing that was supposed to try it out. We wanted to see how he would act there before we took that bigger step. That was D.G.'s plan anyway."

"That's not a bad plan," Mr. Abels said, rubbing his chin.

The real problem, though, was that Chuck was a bully. He always had been. Probably always would be. What could a few kids in a tree fort do about him?

Nonetheless, Everett nodded and said he would try. The moment he said it, though, he knew he'd never be able to convince D.G. What did Chuck want with their tree fort anyway? It was right in the middle of a swamp. It smelled.

His father stood. "I still think I'm going to talk to Jim Davis about this, honey. I don't think our sons need to be engaged in mortal combat."

Everett sucked in his breath. "Wait a minute, Dad. Remember what happened when Chuck was against me because I supposedly ran from the fight? When I tried to talk to Chuck, it only made things worse."

Mr. Abels sighed, obviously thinking. "All right. Let me sleep on it. But any more of these shenanigans, and I'm doing something about it."

Everett felt relieved and got up. He stood there fingering his Coke glass when an idea came to him. "Dad, would you and Mom like to come down and see it—our tree fort, I mean?" He looked from his mother to his father hopefully.

His mother raised her eyebrows and gazed at her husband. "Go down to your tree fort? Is this going to be a new part of the development?"

His father laughed. "Hey, hon, this is a big moment. I had a tree fort when I was a kid." He turned to Everett. "Sure, Ev. Why don't you get all the parents together?"

The moment he said it, though, Everett remembered how D.G. had been so against any parents coming. *Oh, boy,* he thought, *now I've got that problem*.

Later, when they finished dinner, Everett went up to his room. The whole world was stupid. Crazy. If it wasn't Chuck, it was D.G. If it wasn't D.G., it was his dad. It was all so hopeless. When was anything going to go right?

The next morning, Everett spotted D.G. coming down the street. He knew he had to get it out. Maybe if he talked about it before Linc and Tina arrived, they could work it out. He ran up to D.G., smiling until he saw D.G.'s coal black eye. "It looks bad," he said, swallowing and trying not to stare.

"My parents were angry about it, calling Chuck a Nazi and everything. But I calmed them down. They almost weren't going to let me come back. But I told them I'd be all right. I said I had a Christian helping me."

Everett laughed. "What did they say to that?"

"Ah, they didn't like it. But who cares? God is God, isn't He? If He can do something, He will. And if He doesn't, nothing's lost." D.G. paused, then pulled out a slip of paper. "Guess what I found in the paper last night?"

Everett waited.

"A Jersey Buckwolf sighting. Less than five miles from here."

"You're kidding."

D.G. handed Everett the clipping. The headline read, "Sighting of mythical 'Jersey Buckwolf' in Camden County." Everett read:

> Bruce Jamison and his wife reported seeing the mythical Jersey Buckwolf on their property for the last three nights. They own four acres in Marlton, New Jersey, not far from the traditional home of the Jersey Buckwolf, a beast akin to the Abominable Snowman, the Loch Ness Monster, and the Headless Horseman.
>
> The difference between Jamison's and other reports is that Jamison has pictures he snapped on the second and third evenings when he thought the beast might return. The photos are presently in police custody and have not yet been released.

"People are really crazy, even in New Jersey," Everett said.

D.G. laughed, "I know. But it's fun. Keeps the story juices hot."

Everett rolled his eyes. D.G. said, "Let's go down to the tree fort before Chuck has a chance to burn it down."

They hurried toward the creek. Everett still wanted to tell him about the parents visiting the tree fort. Finally, he just came out with it. "D.G., why don't you want our parents to come down and see the tree fort? We could do a great show. Like the Blue Angels do or something."

D.G. stopped up short and stared at Everett. "No way."

"Come on, D.G. That's not good enough. You're not the only one around here. Tina and Linc are for it, too. That's three against . . ."

As D.G.'s cheek muscles flexed, the birthmark reddened. Then just as suddenly, his face changed, and Everett almost thought he would cry. He said, "We can't. We just can't."

"But why?"

D.G. glanced around as though making sure no one was listening. He sighed and bunched up his lips. "Okay, you really want to know?"

"Yeah."

"Because my father's in a wheelchair. We could never get him over."

The wind went right out of Everett. D.G.'s dad was in a wheelchair? He sucked in some air and paused, standing dead still.

"See," D.G. said with a nod. "Now you know."

Everett's stomach balled up, like he had about six donuts in it made of wire. What if his father's brain was damaged and his head leaned over on the side like those people he saw in nursing homes? He scratched the ground with his feet. "I didn't know that. I'm sorry."

But D.G. waved his hand at him. "Hey, it's not too bad. He just can't walk. Paralyzed from the waist down, that's all. From a car accident. It's not like he can't do anything. But we couldn't get him across the rope swing into the woods."

The rope swing? He hadn't really thought about it. He couldn't get his own parents in that way. They'd have to build a bridge or something for all the parents, wouldn't they?

"D.G., we couldn't get any of them in by the rope swing," Everett said with a laugh. "Can you see Linc and Tina's mom swinging over on the rope?"

D.G. laughed.

"What we have to do is build a bridge. That ought to be simple for us to do compared to everything else."

Gazing at Everett, D.G.'s eyes brightened. "I never thought of that." He smiled, "You deserve a mosquito sandwich."

Everett grinned. Sometimes D.G was too smart for himself. His head was so full of inventions, he forgot about normal stuff. "I know we can do it. I even know where we can build it. Look, we can have a big show for all the parents. They'll love it. I know they will. We don't have to show them everything. Just the main things. We can take them through the woods, show them the fort. Put up signs. Have a slingshot exhibition."

D.G.'s eyes were shining. "Hey, that's great. Why didn't I think of it?"

Shrugging sheepishly, Everett was kind of surprised himself. Usually D.G. was out in front of him about five miles.

"Okay," D.G. said, putting out his hand. "It's a deal."

Suddenly a loud bang erupted as they neared the creek. Both boys crouched down instantly. "What was that?" Everett asked.

"Cherry bomb, or a firecracker," D.G. said. "Up that way." He pointed to the north of their rope swing, up toward Chuck's house.

"Don't tell me we're going to have another fight," Everett whispered.

"Let's cross over on the rope swing and come up on the other side. We can stay in the woods."

They swung across without being seen. Then they started up the creek on the woods side. "Be real quiet," D.G. said. "It's only the two of us this time."

15 Almost Done In

They sneaked through the woods toward the sound of the firecrackers. From a distance, Everett saw it was Chuck, this time with four other boys. Besides Stuart and the red-haired boy, there were two other skinny kids, one with a blond crew cut, and the other with lanky brown hair and bony arms. Everett didn't recognize either of them. He and D.G. stopped in the middle of a leafy area where they couldn't be seen.

Several spaced pops sounded and both boys strained to see what was going on. Stuart had a fishing rod in his hand, and something black and snaky wriggled on the ground in front of them. Chuck bent down and lit something. When it exploded, the snaky thing went crazy.

D.G. whispered, "Eels. They're catching eels in the creek and putting firecrackers in their mouths, blowing them up."

"Some fun," Everett said angrily.

They watched helplessly as Stuart yanked another squirming eel out of the murky water. Chuck huddled over the defenseless black thing, shoved a firecracker down its throat and lit a match.

"I'm not going to stand by and watch this," D.G. said.

"What should we do?"

"Tell them we'll report them."

"To who?"

"The police. Or the FBI. Maybe we'll call the White House."

"I'm sure that'll really scare them," Everett said sarcastically.

D.G. scrunched his mouth up. "Yeah, you're right. But maybe we could divert them or something."

"Like throw a rock behind them?"

"Good idea. Can you wing one?"

"Sure." Everett peered at the brown leaf-flecked woods floor. He quickly found a fist-sized stone he knew he could hurl over their heads.

"You throw the stone," D.G. whispered. "Maybe they'll drop the rod and run. Then we can throw the eels back. If there's anything left of them."

It didn't sound particularly bright to Everett. Why would they run just because they heard something behind them? Of course, they might think it was an adult, but if they didn't run and started looking for the source of the stone, he and D.G. could be in real trouble. He hesitated.

D.G. said, "I'll creep up and—what's the matter?"

"What if they come after us? We could both get pounded and I'm already sore and I don't think you need another black eye."

D.G. licked his lips. "We'll have a head start, won't we? They'll have to cross the creek. That will slow them plenty. By that time we could be hundreds of yards away."

"But if they spread out and really search, they could trap us."

Sucking his lip, D.G. said, "Oh, they won't split up. They won't want to be alone out there ready to be ambushed."

"Well, all right." Everett rubbed the rock on his pant leg. Dirt came off on the cut-off shorts.

"Let me get in position, then wing it," D.G. said. He crawled up to the edge of the woods, hidden by the brush and grass on the bank of the creek. Everett moved into position to fling the rock. He wanted to try for a clump of trees directly behind the five boys. That would make plenty of racket.

The stone struck a tree high behind them and bounced—right back into the group of boys, striking Stuart in the back. The wiry boy yelled, and everyone crouched.

Everett ducked down, squatting on the balls of his feet.

"Who is it?" Everett heard Chuck whisper.

"I don't know. That hurt," Stuart answered.

"Is it someone behind us or in the woods?"

Everett didn't move. But he sensed he was about to lose his balance. D.G. stayed still as he looked back at Everett.

"I don't think it's an adult," Stuart said. The boys stood.

"I think it's someone on the other side," Chuck said. "Let's go." He looked up and down the creek. "Just jump in, guys."

As they began wading in the creek, D.G. edged back toward Everett. Then he jumped up. Everett stood.

"Let's peel," D.G. whispered.

As they turned, Everett heard the red-haired boy yell, "There they are."

"It's two of them," Chuck shouted. "Abels and Scarface. Let's move."

Everett yelled, "D.G.—run!"

Both boys sprinted down the trail toward the tree fort. D.G. yelled, "Get off the trail. They'll get us easy."

They plunged into the woods. Brambles and thickets seemed to jump up into their path every way they turned. But they dodged through the woods with fleet feet. Everett didn't hear anyone behind them yet. Spotting a thicket to his left, he panted, "Let's take a look. See where they are."

"No, we can't let them see us. They see us, we're dead. There're five of them." D.G. sped past Everett and they kept going.

They crashed through the woods, finally stopping in another thicket. D.G. squatted down behind a tree and peered out into the woods. Everett stood in the shadow of another tree, out of sight. They listened intently.

Nothing.

Then a thrashing sound. Footsteps. Then a voice, "Spread out. They can run, but they can't hide."

Everett said, "If we're quiet, we can get away. Maybe get around them."

"What if we rush one of them?" D.G. suggested.

Still panting, Everett answered, "Let's go deeper into the woods. We have to think of a plan. But not here."

D.G. agreed. They moved soundlessly to the west away from the tree fort and the creek.

Then someone shouted, "There they are."

Everett's heart seemed to jump into his throat. "All tilt," he cried, and they both put on their best speed, dodging underbrush and brambles. As they ran, Everett suddenly realized what they were doing was stupid. They should be going for the houses. That was where real safety was.

He pumped hard. D.G. legged it right behind him. Their breath came in searing rasps.

Chuck yelled, "First one who pins Frankl gets five bucks." The other boys whooped. They were gaining.

Up ahead, Everett spotted the hill and the rocks. Then he thought of it. The cave. They could hide there. D.G. glanced at Everett, sweat pouring down over his black eye and birthmark. He said with a wheeze, "You thinking what I'm thinking?"

"The cave?"

"Yeah."

"Let's go for it."

Everett murmured to himself, "If we can find it."

As they climbed the hill, they could hear Chuck's gang yelling directions to one another. Then Everett and D.G. reached the rocks. The closest kid—Stuart—was still a good forty yards away. If they kept their heads, they'd get to the cave easily. Then a terrifying thought hit Everett: What if Chuck knew about the cave? They'd be sitting ducks.

With his breath coming hard and the hill growing steeper, Everett prayed silently, "Please, God, don't let him know about the cave. Any of them."

Then he spotted the creek. D.G. was already on it. The smaller boy plunged ahead, then crept in among the rocks. Chuck bellowed behind them like a wolf hot on the scent. But Everett couldn't see the cave. Where was it?

D.G. had moved higher up than Everett. Then suddenly he disappeared. Everett stopped. Just stopped. Craning, he saw the other boys advancing over the rocks, looking for them. Ducking down he lay up against the rock, panting. Where was D.G.? His heart seemed to be bouncing in circles inside his chest.

Suddenly, he felt a hand on his arm. He twisted around in terror. It was D.G. "Come on. It's right here."

They were inside in less than five seconds. They both

scrambled through the front part of the cave on either side of the creek.

"Let's keep going in," D.G. said. "Deep. They won't be able to see us in the dark." Then he made a helpless sound. "I forgot, they have matches."

Everett whispered, "Maybe they won't be able to find the cave entrance."

"That's our only hope," D.G. answered.

Everett stared into the darkness, then back at the entrance hole. Already he could hear voices outside. D.G. turned around. With the light from the hole, Everett could see his sweaty face and the fear on it. "Come on. We'll hide deeper, just in case they look in."

They heard a voice resound outside the hole, "Where did they go? They were right here somewhere."

D.G. murmured, "Don't you wish you knew?"

As they crawled deeper into the cave, the ceiling and the floor V-ed closer together over the stream. It had gotten so dark, Everett couldn't see his hand in front of his face. Then D.G. said, "Didn't Seth say something about another connecting cave?"

Instantly, Everett remembered. "Yeah, maybe we can find it."

He sensed D.G. was turning around, looking. "It's got to be right here, away from the spring. Grab my shoe."

Everett groped around in the darkness. His hand struck water. It made him shiver. A moment later, he found D.G.'s leg. D.G. sneezed.

"Okay. Hold my ankle, and just keep behind me. We'll be okay."

They crept along through the cave. There were still no sounds of anyone behind them. Then they heard one of the boys yell, "Hey, look, a hole. A cave."

Closing his eyes, Everett prayed again that there really was a passageway to the other side. Another voice called, "I bet they're in there."

As they turned the corner, the darkness only deepened. He heard the boys scrabbling around the hole. *Lord, let there be another cave*. Then he saw it: a glimmer of light ahead.

There really was another way out. D.G. crawled toward it. The voices were clearly coming from the mouth of the cave. Everett figured Chuck would probably light a match before going in, so that would take some time, and probably all of them would follow him. By that time, he and D.G. would be long gone.

Hopefully.

In less than a minute, they reached the other mouth of the cave. It was smaller, less visible than the other one. It would be a tight fit. D.G. paused. "We've got to make sure they can't see us."

Everett eyed the hole. It looked about the size of basketball.

D.G. held up his hand. "Just listen."

Behind them the echo of voices indicated they were inside the cave.

"I think they're all in," D.G. said.

He leaned toward the hole. "Seth couldn't get out of this baby," he said. He stuck his head out.

Everett waited uneasily in the darkness, straining to hear any other noises besides Chuck and the others. They were clamoring in the cave now. "Yo—Frankl! You in here? Here, little Jew boy!"

D.G. pushed through the hole. As his belly reached the middle, the light went out completely. Everett shivered. *Hurry up, D.G.*

Then he was out. D.G. stuck his head back in. "Come on. We're clear."

Everett was bigger than D.G., and it felt tight. He had to extend his arms over his head and keep his face in the dirt. He pushed with his sneakers. His hips reached the hole. He scrabbled for a hold. Nothing. He was stuck. His head was almost into the light.

Then D.G. took his hands. "Let me pull you."

As Everett's hips scraped on the sides of the hole, D.G. pulled and grunted.

Everett winced as his waist ground on the hole. He couldn't move. Then D.G. jerked his arms with all his might. It felt like they came out of their sockets. But he was free. He wriggled out.

"That was tight," Everett said as they squatted, peering over the rocks in the direction of the other cave. "Chuck won't be able to get out that way, though."

Their faces were covered with dirt, their clothes wet

and grubby from the springwater. "Head right for the creek," D.G. said. "Then we'll be at the houses. They won't attack us in broad daylight."

None of the boys was in sight. D.G. and Everett hurried silently down the hill, into the woods and toward the creek. In five minutes, they reached it. Beautiful, people-filled houses lined the street.

"We're home free," D.G. said with a pant.

They waded across the creek without taking their sneakers off, then ran up the hill to the street. They were about three streets from Everett's home.

"I bet they're still in the cave, wondering how we disappeared," D.G. said.

Everett began to breath easily for the first time. "That was close, D.G. Too close. Chuck is going to be madder than ever."

"That's why we won't give him another opening. We're going to scare the stuffing out of that guy."

"We are?"

D.G. smiled craftily. "Yes, we are."

"But how?"

D.G. pulled the article out of his pocket again. "We're going to have Chuck Davis and his friends meet the Jersey Buckwolf."

16 In Need of an Actor

"How are we gonna do that?" Everett asked, brushing the dirt from his knees. In the light, D.G.'s black eye looked even worse.

D.G. rubbed his nose and wiped his fist over his thick eyebrows. "I don't know yet. But you said Chuck used to collect stuff about the Jersey Buckwolf, right?"

"He had a whole scrapbook. Even his father had some things from when he was little. They're real superstitious and everything. They even went on camping trips to try and photograph it. He used to show me the scrapbook. He had clippings and all sorts of things." Even as Everett talked, ideas were pouring into his head. "I mean, none of the pictures was ever really clear, but they believed it."

The pair hurried up the street toward Fork Way where Everett and Linc and Tina lived. The heat stifled them. As Everett breathed in deeply, the air almost seared his chest.

"Maybe we could do something with Whip and Bump," he said suddenly. "Tina might be able to teach them some special trick. Maybe we could dress them up somehow."

D.G. shook his head up and down. "Now you're thinking. The hard part is the bait. How do we get him down there? I mean, this is the way we could scare him and his friends out of the woods permanently. If we can make them all believe the Jersey Buckwolf roams these woods, we could have the whole place to ourselves."

Everett shivered with prickles of delight. Would he ever love to see Chuck run from a setup like that.

"We've got to lay some groundwork," D.G. said. He kicked at a stone in the road. "Fast. Chuck won't be sitting on it this time. He'll be coming back every day."

Everett hadn't thought of that. Until now, their encounters of Chuck had been occasional. But now it was bound to be a major problem. They reached Linc and Tina's house. Their mother's car was still gone. But just as they turned to head toward Everett's home, Mrs. Watterson pulled into the driveway. Tina and Linc jumped out.

"What on earth happened to you?" Tina cried as she hurried over to them.

"We had a little run-in with Chuck," D.G. said. Mrs.

Watterson gave the boys a fast look, said hello, then told Linc and Tina to come in for lunch. D.G. explained what had happened.

"It's going to be a never-ending battle," Linc said. "We'll either have to forget the tree fort or go somewhere else. We can't win with five of them."

D.G. told them about his idea with the Jersey Buckwolf and showed them the newspaper clipping. Tina and Linc read with interest.

"After lunch, come on over to my house," Everett said. "We can work out some plans. Then we can talk to Seth, see what he thinks. He'll help, I bet."

Everyone agreed.

That afternoon they gathered in Everett's basement for a "council of war." Tina and Linc already brimmed over with ideas. They batted around thoughts of one of them dressing up as the Jersey Buckwolf, but D.G. nixed that, saying it wouldn't work because they were all too small and not fast enough.

They kept coming back to Whip and Bump. Two Jersey Buckwolves. Or one and his son. It would be easy to rig up some gear for them, perhaps a horn for their heads—Seth had several—a mane, and a hairy coat to drape over their bodies. At night they'd be just spooky enough to scare Chuck and his friends but good. The way they "choreographed" it, as D.G. said, was critical. They had to plan it in detail for maximum effect and so that it looked like a real appearance. However, getting them down there at the right moment might be impossible.

"First, we have to talk to Seth," D.G. said. "I think he'll go along with it—especially if it's all done in good fun."

Everyone agreed.

That evening before dinner they talked to Seth. The old construction worker said, "Awful hard to pull off, kids. It'd be almost like a movie set. I'd put my eyes on something else. And Whip and Bump could never be trained in time. I've had to work with them for months just to get them to learn the few tricks they know."

"But what can we do?" D.G.'s voice was almost a wail.

"Power of the imagination's where I'd start," Seth said. "But remember, you want to do right by the Lord in this."

"Chuck doesn't," Linc answered.

"And he doesn't answer to you about that," Seth said. "He answers to God. Just set your beans on the things above and you'll be all right."

No one looked very happy about Seth's answer, and D.G. plowed ahead with more questions about scaring Chuck and the others out of the woods. He seemed set on it, and finally Seth wiped his forehead and said, "Each of us got to do what we got to do. I don't think it'll work, but you can try. I'd just caution you to remember to pray to the good Lord and He'll do something, guaranteed."

"Then why hasn't He done it yet?" D.G. answered with frustration.

Seth smiled. "If I could answer that one, I could solve ever' problem ever was. But God works in His own time. He has to set things up right to bring off what He intends to bring off. I'd say, do what you can and leave the rest to Him. But I'd encourage you once more to really pray about it."

After all the discussion, D.G. finally said, "Well, we do need one thing for sure, whatever happens?"

"What's that?" Everett asked.

"Time."

That evening they got it. Everett was out for a walk with his sister and brother and passed Chuck's house. He had been praying silently about the things Seth said, and he just wasn't sure what to do. D.G. appeared to be set on some plan to scare Chuck. It all looked improbable and impossible.

Then he spotted Mr. Davis out in the driveway loading up their station wagon. Everett said hello. "Are you going somewhere?"

"Two weeks at the beach," Mr. Davis said. Chuck wasn't outside. Everett remembered that the Davis family usually took a vacation each summer at Somers Point where Chuck's uncle had a house on the beach.

"Everyone's going?" Everett asked again.

"Yes," Mr. Davis said, out of breath. He was a tall man, with a friendly face. He was usually friendly to Everett, even since Chuck and he had not been friends.

"Have a good one," Everett said as they continued up the street. "Just what we needed," he murmured. "Now we've got two weeks to get everything ready."

It seemed like a miracle. Maybe God was answering their prayer.

That night as he lay in bed, he tried to think through all the things that could possibly go wrong. The plan D.G. had outlined sounded hokey. Chuck would not only laugh in their faces, he'd club them but good.

On the other hand, if Seth would let them use Whip and Bump for something, that might be enough to keep Chuck away. Knowing that they were friends with two toothy Doberman pinschers around could scare anyone.

He thought about the Jersey Buckwolf again. He knew it was all made up. But why did people believe that stuff? Why did Chuck believe it? Sure, it made good sitting-around-the-campfire story material. But could they really scare Chuck enough to keep him away? Or would it only pull him in all the more?

Everett fell into a deep sleep and awoke from a vivid dream in which the woods around the tree fort filled with smoke and huge green eyes surrounded them all. It gave him the jitters at first, but it faded soon after he woke up.

When the group learned Chuck would be gone for two weeks, they were ecstatic. "Now we can bring it off," D.G. exclaimed. "That's more than enough time for the show and for the defense measures."

The foursome threw themselves into their efforts. They found an open place north of the tree fort along the creek to build a bridge for D.G.'s dad to cross on. They used flat boards they'd found discarded at several house work sites. They found so many, in fact, they ended up with a pile of leftovers stacked between two trees to the front right of the tree fort. Many of them had nails driven through them, so they had to be careful. Someone could trip on a root, come face down in that pile, and lose an eye.

After that, they built up the tree fort, camouflaged it with tree leaves and branches, and practiced their slinging. D.G. quickly came up with more defensive measures. He found an old fishing net in his garage. He envisioned a net that would drop over people at the pull of a switch on the top tier of the tree fort. They nailed ladders into the trees to set it up. They also built a third platform above the two they already had. It was at least twenty feet off the ground, and they could see from it all the way to the creek behind Chuck's house.

Getting the release on the net was difficult. But D.G. devised a way to stretch it out under the trees in the air and hold it in place by four wooden pins on strings. They stretched string from the pins to the top of the tree fort. When someone pulled all four strings at once, the net plunked down evenly.

After working at it for several days, they'd managed to string the net up over the area quickly and fix it in place by the pins without strain. Some cork buoys attached to it made it fall swiftly. D.G. dyed it green so that it became invisible under the leafy bows of the trees whose branches didn't spread out till they were fifteen or twenty feet in the air.

Everett set up a number of party-popper booby traps in the woods. So long as it didn't rain, he knew they'd be good alert devices to warn them of any intruders. Someone coming by would trip a line connected to the pull on the party popper. By making it explode inside a bucket, it made an incredibly loud noise. D.G. explained that this was their "early warning" system much like the way the U.S.A. had detectors around Russia in case of nuclear attack.

They stashed water balloons all over the woods. "We'll soak them but good," D.G. explained. The balloons had a washable black dye in them that would create a huge blotch on their clothing.

They talked about digging a long ditch in the middle of the open area and filling it with goo from the marsh. But they decided to get everything ready for their parents before Sunday. Afterward, they could work on the ditch. They did dig a number of potholes, concealing them under a matting of leaves and sticks. They hauled swamp goo and dropped it into the bottom of each hole.

D.G. finally said he was designing several "real secret" weapons he knew would make their enemies run in a major battle. He didn't tell them what they were. "But," he said, "they'd only be used in a last-ditch effort." Everett wondered what these were, but he decided not to question D.G. about them.

They still had the problem of getting Chuck down there at the right time. How they would bring that about, no one had any idea, and if D.G. did he wasn't saying. He only told them, "I'm working on the logistics," whatever that meant.

From the start, Tina and Linc had talked to their parents about the show, and so had Everett. It was agreed everyone would come on Sunday afternoon at fourteen hundred hours to the Wattersons' backyard for a cookout.

However, D.G. stayed nervous about it. He wasn't sure whether his father and mother would come. He told Everett the Thursday before the show, "I'm asking them tonight. Keep your fingers crossed."

Everett went home that evening full of hope.

D.G. called at nine. After answering, he was silent and Everett waited. He could tell D.G. was going to spring it on him.

"Okay—are they coming?"

D.G. yelled into the phone. "*Yessssss!*"

He'd never heard D.G. so excited.

After a few minutes of talk, Everett signed off and awaited Sunday with a surge of happiness in his heart. Once everyone saw the tree fort, it would become real and important in a way it had never yet been.

That Friday, the foursome planned out a whole program. They prepared everything that afternoon, put up targets, checked the bridge, and waited for Sunday.

In the meantime, they also made more plans for building an interest in the Jersey Buckwolf on Chuck's part. They came up with variations galore, but in the end D.G. put together what he called "The Jersey Buckwolf Fan Club Campaign." He was sure it would lure Chuck and his friends to the tree fort at the right time.

Or so they all thought.

When Everett arrived at the Wattersons' with his parents, brother, and sister, Linc took him aside. "Do you think D.G. will really come?"

"Yes. He'll be here. Don't worry." But Everett watched the side of the house for signs of the Frankls pulling into the driveway.

Mrs. Watterson had prepared sandwich meats, potato salad, coleslaw, and soft drinks for everyone in the backyard around the pool. Everett's mother and father talked to Mr. Watterson genially by the picnic table. Everett thought they looked very up-to-date in their blue jeans and matching T-shirts with Him and Her stenciled on the front. Linc and Tina's parents wore shorts and light shirts. Mrs. Watterson bounced about spreading cheer and patting heads, but even she looked worried. Was D.G. going to show?

Then at five of two, a blue van pulled up at the driveway. D.G. popped out. His black eye had dribbled away to some purple marks by his nose. He waved to Linc, Tina, and Everett.

D.G. slid the side door open. An elevatorlike contraption buzzed and descended with a grating noise. Then a big man with a thick, black beard and a skullcap rumbled onto the deck in a wheelchair. D.G. operated the controls. "Like lifting a bulldozer shovel," he yelled, grinning.

"Let's get this circus on the road, Dodai!" Mr. Frankl boomed. He wore a three-piece blue suit and looked unready for anything the woods had to offer.

Everett's father came around the edge of the house. "Need any help?" he said. No one said anything. They all stood there transfixed. Mr. Frankl just laughed with a deep, bellowing haw-haw. "What do you think this is—Barnum and Bailey? Where's the lox and bagels?"

"I'm Tom Abels," Everett's father said, extending his hand.

"Joseph Frankl," thundered the big man. "This is my wife, Sarah, and you know Dodai." D.G. looked uncomfortable, but smiled anyway.

Mrs. Frankl patted her gray dress and gazed about with small green eyes. Her hair was gray and curly. Then she waved her hand toward D.G. "Well, lead the way, Dodai. Don't make us stand here perspiring in the sun."

Quickly, Mr. Watterson and Everett's dad hefted the wheelchair and lifted it over the front stairs and the stoop. Soon the parents began talking about what parents always talked about while the foursome gathered at a corner of the pool.

Everett whispered to D.G., "Do you think we can really get your dad across? I mean, that wheelchair looks pretty big."

"If he falls in, he falls in," D.G. said with a chuckle. "He might like it."

Mrs. Watterson herded everyone to the picnic table and soon the group was snarfing kosher corned beef and cheese sandwiches with gusto. When things simmered down, Mr. Frankl suddenly said, "Well, where is this skyscraper my Gamaliel has built? On with it. Get me there before I expire from too much *goyisch lechem* and *chemah.* That's Gentile bread and cheese, if you want a translation. Now on with it."

The bridge was rickety, but with the help of the dads, they got everyone including Mr. Frankl across into the woods. D.G. ushered them all into a semicircle and explained the first step of their expedition. "Before we actually show you Fort Dayan, we'll do a brief commando exercise at the rope bridge forty yards down the creek. I and my three compatriots will show you that real commandos do not rely on wooden bridges to cross a river."

Mr. Frankl shouted, "Dodai Gamaliel Frankl—spokesman of the people!"

Everett looked at Tina and Linc. They really did call D.G. by those names! As they walked down the trail toward the rope swing, Mrs. Frankl stopped D.G., and said, "Dodai, what's this name 'D.G.'? Have you been using an alias?"

Gulping, D.G. escaped to the head of the crowd, issuing orders. Everett overheard Mrs. Frankl remark to his mother, "That boy can't live with anything given to him. He must change it all."

After they demonstrated their rope swing prowess with even Mr. Watterson trying it, they followed the trail back to the fort. Mr. Frankl's wheelchair bumped and creaked along the path. The smell of the swamp diminished as they entered the forest, but it remained rank. Then D.G. hoisted the ladder and let it down by the hidden rope. "This is our secret way of getting into the fort," he announced.

Everett's father walked around it, watching the movements from different angles. After a few minutes, he smiled and shook his head. "Ingenious! One of you is a real engineer."

D.G.'s eyes didn't flicker. He said, "Everett made the ladder, Tina figured out how to hide the secret string, and Linc . . ." He paused. "Linc practiced his front flips in the yard while we did the work."

Mr. and Mrs. Watterson laughed especially hard at their athletic son.

The foursome climbed into the tree fort and took their stations on the three floors. D.G. took the top floor with his legs parted and his hands behind his back. "An important moment in the proceedings has come," he said, "that moment when Fort Dayan will demonstrate its real firepower."

The little group of parents and kids stood underneath them, looking up with some wonder. Everett watched D.G.'s father. He kept plucking at his beard. Mrs. Frankl laid her right hand on his shoulder.

"First," D.G. said, "you will notice that we picked our way into this region very carefully. That's because there are a number of 'swamp whamps' around you. If any of you initiated hostile action against us, you would soon find you were surrounded by a series of muck pits as deadly as a cobra's basket."

Everett and Tina stifled grins, keeping rigidly at attention.

D.G. went on, "I bid you not to move in any direction lest you end up to your eyeballs, or at least your knees, in goo."

The mothers made faces and Lance yelled, "Where is it? Where is it?" But D.G. waved him off. "That's for us to know and you not to find out."

He directed Mrs. Watterson to take four steps to the left. Everett could see the string tied to a party popper between the two trees. D.G. coaxed, "Walk slowly now. Straight. That's it."

BAM!

Everyone jumped and a confetti of stringy paper fired into the air. Jillie screamed.

"Claymore mine," D.G. said. "Actually, a party-popper explosive device. But deadly on the nerves."

After going through the other demonstrations, D.G. announced the *pièce de résistance*—which he explained meant "the main course." Tina climbed to the top floor of the fort. D.G. shimmied down a nearby tree they sometimes used like a quick exit fire pole and stood in the middle of the group. "Don't be afraid," he intoned. "This will not hurt. But I advise you to cover your heads."

Mrs. Frankl cried, "This had better not ruin my hairdo, Dodai."

Still at attention, D.G. intoned, "We've accounted for every possibility. There will be no mussed hairdos." He looked up at Tina. "Let 'er rip."

Tina jerked the four strings at once. There was a pause. Everyone looked up. Then the net plummeted down over them, the six cork buoys clunking to the ground around them. Lance and Jillie squealed with excitement. From the tree fort they looked like butterflies caught in a huge butterfly net.

Mr. Frankl yelled, "If you don't get me out of this contraption, I'll take out my pipe knife and cut it all to smithereens." Mrs. Frankl, though, shook her head. "Do you always have to be so dramatic, Dodai?"

"I think it's still got a bit of a fish smell to it," Everett's father said. "You haven't been using this thing in the creek, have you?"

After everyone pulled the net off and the leaves and debris out of their hair, D.G. announced the *coup de grace*—he pronounced it "coop de grayse"—which, he said, meant "the finishing blow."

"Now for the slingshot contest." He hurried behind a tree and brought out a bull's-eye that even Everett hadn't known about. It was stretched across a hula hoop and attached at the corners by strings. D.G. placed the bull's-eye about thirty feet away against a tree.

He laid a stone in the sling wad and told everyone to stand back. The bull's-eye had a large red center, with a yellow ring around it, and then a blue ring. D.G. swung the sling around his head. Everett noticed the parents duck down. But he knew D.G.'s aim was good. He let the stone go. It smacked through the paper in the lower circle of yellow, leaving a round, even hole.

Everett stepped up. He wasn't sure he could even hit the target anywhere, let alone in the red. But he whirled the sling and let go. The stone struck the yellow, on the top-side.

Tina walked to the line, bowed, and said to the gathering, "Girls can do this, too." She fixed the stone in the pouch and whirled it deftly. With a plunk, her stone shot a hole in the upper blue, not far from Everett's hole.

Finally, Linc stood to fire. He said nothing, going carefully about putting his stone into the pouch, then winging it. With a yell, he punctured the red, the first one to do so.

Everyone cheered, but D.G. held up his hands. "Three points for red, two for yellow, and one for blue. It's now two-two-one-three. But we have another target."

Scurrying again behind the trees, D.G. dangled out a second target. This one was smaller, also on a hula hoop. He hung the target in the same position. The four all took their shots. D.G. hit another yellow. Everett and Tina pricked holes in the blue. And Linc missed altogether. As they shot at the different targets, D.G. kept looking at his father as though expecting him to say something, but Mr. Frankl said nothing and peacefully smoked his pipe.

Finally, D.G. brought out a frying pan. Immediately, Mrs. Frankl yelled, "I've been looking for that for a week!"

"Mom," D.G. chided, "it was an old rusty one in the garage."

"Rusty, my eye," Mrs. Frankl said. But Everett could tell she was amused. She said to Everett's mother, "The boy finds everything in the garage."

D.G. hung it by a string from a branch. With a careful push, he swung it back and forth like a clock pendulum. "Whoever hits this is champion," D.G. said, looking at his father mysteriously. But the bearded man's eyes didn't flicker.

Everett squinted and swung the sling slowly over his

head, gradually gaining speed. Twice he began to release, then stopped. Finally he let it go. The stone struck the handle, knocking the pan in its arc. But he missed the pan. Everyone groaned.

Next Tina stepped to the line. She whirled a long time, then pitched the stone with a sharp, whipping motion.

The stone struck the tree, missing the pan completely.

After that, D.G. moved to the line, his face confident, his eyes slits. Even his birthmark seemed to have receded deep into his face. Everett set the pan swinging. D.G. paced and worked to get the right position. Finally, he placed the stone in the pouch. He whirled it over his head, and released. The stone nicked the side of the pan, making it spin.

Several parents clapped, but D.G. motioned to Linc. "Your turn."

Linc came up to the line. He didn't do any of the dramatics as the others had done. He simply slung the stone. And missed.

D.G. was about to speak, but Mr. Frankl said, "I believe I'll take a shot. In fact, I'll take three."

A murmur arose from the group, but D.G. smiled and handed him his slingshot. "Go ahead, Papa. Let's see what you can do." Everett sensed that something fishy was up. Did Mr. Frankl really know how to do this?

Fixing his pipe in his teeth, Mr. Frankl wheeled over the leaves to the line. He said, "I'll take two practice shots first. I need to get the range and see how well this little mechanism works. It's been quite a long time."

Everyone stepped back. Mr. Frankl looked rather ungainly in his wheelchair, but the moment he began whirling the sling, Everett could tell he knew precisely what he was doing. He spun it twice without firing. Then he scrutinized the stones D.G. had handed him. Finally, he selected one.

"Let it swing," he said. "But remember, this is just practice. My real shot will be the third one."

D.G. set the pan swinging back and forth. Mr. Frankl whirled, then released the stone. It sailed over the top of the pan and banged into a tree on the other side. Everett could tell it had been a good shot. A foot lower, it might have struck the pan dead center.

Mr. Frankl loaded a second stone. This time he pushed himself up higher in the wheelchair and adjusted his pillow. He was careful, methodical. He was obviously enjoying the attention, blowing out rings of smoke between each shot.

He whirled the sling again. Then with a sudden ferocity, he let it go. This time it shimmered a foot below the pan. Right in line with the pan, though. Everett felt the tension building. Could Mr. Frankl do it?

The big man took the third stone. Even the woods grew quiet. He loaded the stone carefully, after rubbing it over and over in his palm. Then he took a puff from his pipe and turned to D.G. "Take my pipe, Gamaliel."

D.G. took it from his mouth. Everett stood at the pan and pushed it into a quick arc. Mr. Frankl slowly, methodically took aim. He began to twirl the sling. His arm was going furiously. Everett watched his face and recognized that same passionate excitement he always saw in D.G. Mr. Frankl let the stone go with a yell. "For Israel!"

BING! The stone rang the pan like a bell.

There was an amazed pause. Then everyone broke out cheering. Everett smiled. He'd never seen anything like this. He said to D.G., "How did he know how to do it?"

D.G. grinned. "I taught him everything he knows."

"You mean, I taught you everything you know," said Mr. Frankl with a wink.

Everyone congratulated Mr. Frankl. All the parents remarked what a wonderful show it was. After the foursome took bows, D.G. led them back. Mr. Abels announced he was going over by the rope, but would meet them at the bridge to help Mr. Frankl across. Everett went over ahead of his dad and waited on the other side. The tall brown-haired man swished across like a master trapeze artist. When he jumped down on the other side, Everett's mouth dropped open. "I didn't know you could do that."

Mr. Abels rubbed Everett's scalp. "I was a kid once, too, you know." Then he called back to his wife. "Come on, honey, show them your stuff."

Everett watched with even greater astonishment as his mother sailed over lightly and hopped down on the other side as if she'd done it eight times that day. She brushed Everett's hair, too. "Didn't think your old lady could do it, did you?"

As they walked, Mrs. Abels put her arm over Everett's shoulder and gave him a quick kiss. "It was a fun time, honey."

His cheeks burned. But he felt good. He felt really good.

Before the four split up that afternoon, D.G. said, "All right. Now the fun's over. We have a week to prepare for Chuck's return. Tomorrow we begin the real work. Get your minds ready."

All that night Everett tossed in bed. It had been such a great day. But he kept dreaming about huge horned creatures with blue eyes running through the woods and stomping on the tree fort. Just as everything came crashing down he woke up.

He fell back to sleep, but later he awakened and listened to the birds. Why couldn't Chuck simply let them alone? They'd made all these elaborate preparations, but anything could go wrong. The whole plot could fall apart as easily as wet Kleenex. As he lay in the dark, he could imagine Chuck's fist smashing into his face. Every time he closed his eyes, there it was. That fist. Smashing. Smashing.

Then his mother was shaking him. "Everett! Everett! You're having a bad dream. Wake up!"

He shot up. His pajamas were wet with sweat. He looked at her. She bent over him, looking anxiously into his face.

"It was just a dream, honey. Go back to sleep. It's only six o'clock."

He looked up into her eyes. Those gray, unblinking, so-sure eyes. Had she ever been afraid of someone? Did she know what it was like to be afraid?

She kissed him on his forehead. "It's all right. It was just a dream."

He watched her close the door. But he knew Chuck would come back. There would be a fight. People would get hurt. And then he'd come back again. And again. Until the tree fort was destroyed. Until everyone was hurt and destroyed. And he'd still keep coming. There was no stopping him.

Tears seared into his eyes as he looked across the space that separated his bed from his brother's bed. Why couldn't there just be peace?

Then an alarm buzzed and he jumped up. After rubbing his eyes, he crawled out of bed and went to the bathroom.

In the morning light, things didn't feel so bad.

Monday was a beautiful, sunny morning with a cool breeze blowing. When they all arrived at the fort, D.G. was already making preparations. He explained to them, "First we dig that ditch and muck trap. And get the net set back up. Make sure there is plenty of ammo in the ammo dumps. Plus we need to hide ammo dumps around the fort in the woods in case we're driven from the fort and have to go underground. Then . . . "

Everett already felt nervous. Would any of D.G.'s ideas work? Or would it all be like a grade-B movie with grade-D see-through special effects? Worst of all, it might just anger Chuck all the more. He'd want blood—if he didn't laugh at them at first.

And still, what could they do? They'd tried to make peace. That hadn't worked. But were they just to give him the tree fort and leave? Not even that would work. Chuck would keep coming at them—in school, on the street.

There was nothing they could do. They couldn't make peace. They couldn't give up some part of the forest, because the only part Chuck would want was their part. The only thing left to do was dig in, make a defense, fight back. Or give him such a scare that he'd never be back.

As they began to work, Everett felt more hopeless than ever. He kept listening for that crack of a stick and that rustle through the trees. He found himself praying repeatedly, "What are You doing, Lord?"

Still, they worked all morning. Linc and Everett hacked out the pit underneath the net and dug toward the mire. Meanwhile, D.G. climbed the trees and maneuvered the net back into place. Tina stocked the ammo dumps in the fort with plastic eggs filled with raw egg and a few dyed-water balloons. She gathered stones and carved out secret caches around the area and down by the creek.

On Tuesday, they broke through to the marsh. Nothing moved at first. But with some help from the shovels, they filled up the pit and the alley to it. D.G. carefully covered it all with a thick bed of leaves. It was invisible.

Each afternoon, Seth let Tina bring the dogs down for a visit. But Seth was very firm that they were not to let Whip and Bump attack anyone. They were to come and get him if they needed help.

Still Seth assured them God would work if they kept praying. Worst thing that could happen was that Chuck wouldn't be scared off, and they'd have to come up with some other way to deal with him. But "That's life," he said.

Then on Wednesday, D.G. unfolded the whole plan. As D.G. outlined, it sounded like a movie script. But Everett had been to several fun houses that youth workers had created and they were fairly effective. It wouldn't be hard to pull it off. But whether Chuck and his friends would actually run was another question.

"And how do we get him down to this woods, to this place?" Linc asked.

"My Uncle Lemuel!" D.G. said. "He's my father's

brother. He runs a small Jewish newspaper in Camden. But he also has a side business."

Everyone waited until Everett said, "Okay, what's the side business?" He noticed his heart had begun to pound with excitement.

D.G. explained, "He'll take the regular issue of most any newspaper, including our local paper, and put you on the cover. Your picture, or whatever. It's a gimmicky kind of thing. You've probably seen operations like it at Atlantic City on the Boardwalk. People really go for it. They get a story on the cover with all the regular stuff as well. It's real easy because it's done through computerization. Anyway, I think I can get him to do it for us for free."

"You mean, he'd put us on the cover of the *Camden Courier?*" Linc, Tina, and Everett said it together.

"Not for real. Just a fake version. But I think . . ." D.G. laid out the whole plan. It sounded farfetched, even insane, but in a way, it would be fun. Even if it didn't work, it would get a good laugh. Chuck might even find it funny.

Then D.G. pulled a tape recorder out of his knapsack. "This is what it'll sound like," he said. He pushed the button. An eerie recording came on with all sorts of weird noises, including these wolflike howls and another clicking sound like teeth gnashing together or even claws. As Everett listened, it raised the hair on his neck. Just listening to that tape in the deep woods at night would be enough to scare anyone. D.G. said he'd fabricated it from some old horror movie videos his father had.

D.G. said, "I may even be able to work it up with two tape recorders. At different points in the woods, it could be real scary." Everett swallowed with amazement and prickles of fear jetting up and down his spine.

"Then the climax," D.G. said. "The last thing is that we paint pairs of green eyes in fluorescent paint all over the woods. As we shine our lights at certain places, they'll light up. The tapes will be on with all the whispery noises saying, 'Get them, Get them,' and it'll be like we're surrounded. Everett and I yell and hightail it out of there. It'll be bold, black terror."

D.G. looked around at the other three. It sounded like *Raiders of the Lost Ark* or something. How did D.G. dream this up?

"After that," D.G. said, "everyone meets back at the tree fort area and we have a good laugh as Chuck and the others scram home."

Everett sat there stunned and amazed. This was incredible. The whole time he'd been listening, the back of his neck prickled with excitement and terror. It looked perfect. It might even work. At least with someone like Chuck.

Still, Everett thought, there were still plenty of "ifs." If Chuck bit. If he got interested enough to come down. If he showed up at the right place. If everything went correctly. Maybe then, just maybe he would be scared for good.

Maybe.

It was a mighty big maybe.

Afterward D.G. discussed other strategies. He drew a map on the forest floor with a sharp stick. They could use all the other defensive measures in case of a real confrontation. But hopefully that wouldn't be necessary.

Then, D.G. went to his knapsack. "Finally, the big guns. Believe me, I don't want to use these. But this is like our nuclear threat." He fished some peashooters out of the knapsack, then a small vial of a white powder, and two other plastic bottles without labels.

D.G. laid the peashooters down next to the bottle of powder and some small cloth circles. "You've all seen and used peashooters, right?"

Everyone nodded enthusiastically.

Picking up one of the cloth wads and the bottle, D.G. explained, "This stuff is a special chemical that cops use. They might put some in a store where kids have been shoplifting. When you get this stuff on your skin and you sweat a little, the chemical turns purple. Ugly purple. And it won't come off for several days, even a week. The chemical—it's called 'Catch 'em Purplehanded'—my father has used it in his work at the bakery when they had some stealing going on. The crook tried to cover it up by wearing gloves, but they got him."

D.G. took out another pouch of white stuff. "This is just flour. But I'll show you how it works. First, we warn Chuck what he's up against. Then we do this." D.G. packed a little flour into the middle of the patch, then loaded it into the peashooter. "Stand up, Linc."

Linc stood up.

"Move back about five feet."

Linc moved.

D.G. put the peashooter up to his mouth. He blew. The wad zipped out, opened, and Linc stood there with a patch of white powder on his neck and cheek. He brushed it out of his eyes.

D.G. said, "Now imagine that in the middle of a fight, we use this on our enemy. He ends up with purple splotches all over him."

"Won't that just make him madder?" Everett asked.

"Sure. But we can wear him down, too. The main thing is, we keep them on the edge, never knowing what to expect next. And no one gets hurt."

Everett waited, his heart pounding. This was like real war, he thought. Didn't some countries use chemical weapons in war?

"One more thing, and we definitely don't want to have to use this," D.G. said, holding up a bottle. "It can really hurt. I mean it only as a threat. I probably wouldn't ever really use it. But it has great scare power."

"What is it?" Everett asked.

D.G. held up the bottle. "All we have to do is spray some in his face and he'll stop for good."

"What on earth is it?" Tina said impatiently.

"Ammonia," D.G. said. "You know, for cleaning and stuff."

Everyone sat dead still, barely daring to breathe.

D.G. nodded. "You get ammonia on your skin and it burns. And it'll blind you if you don't get it out of your eyes. I don't ever intend to use it. Unless . . ." He didn't finish the sentence.

"That stuff is really dangerous," Everett said.

"And so are Chuck Davis and his friends," D.G. said. He gazed around at everyone. "Look, we don't want to lose this battle, right? We always have to have something in reserve. We don't really intend to use it. But we can threaten it, just to keep the little dictators like Chuck under control."

"But what if the fight gets really bad?" Tina asked. She glanced at Everett and Linc worriedly. "What if he uses it on us?"

D.G. shook his head. "We'll just have to take precautions. All you have to do is wash it off quickly, anyway. It's not like it's lethal."

Everett swallowed, realizing D.G. was probably right. Long before they ever got to the ammonia, Chuck would have been destroyed by all the other stuff. But what if it came down to it? What if D.G. was really going to use it?

He told himself not to think about that possibility. It wouldn't happen. If no one else, God wouldn't let it happen.

D.G. finally said, "If it comes down to it, we can always leave. Forget the tree fort. Stick to the neighborhood streets where people can see us at all times so that Chuck wouldn't dare start something in broad daylight."

"You make it sound like a prison," Everett said.

"Right," said D.G. "That's exactly where he's got us. So this is the best we can do. We have a right to defend ourselves."

It was frustrating. Everett thought about what his mom and Seth had said about loving your enemies and praying for them. He wasn't sure how to bring it up. If he should. But then he was saying it.

D.G. shook his head adamantly. "Haven't we tried that? We can't defend ourselves that way. I can see it now in the 1967 war. The headlines read, 'Israelis send love notes, roses, and kisses to Arabs. Everyone very happy.' "

Even Everett got that one. He sighed, "But what about what Seth said?"

All three of them fixed their eyes on D.G. Everett really wanted an answer. Because if the Christian way didn't work here, it wouldn't work anywhere.

Sighing, D.G. said, "Well, the problem is, Chuck is not acting like a person who wants to believe and follow God, right? So how do you deal with them? Do you try to do it God's way with people who don't even care about God and His way?"

It made some sense, but something about it wasn't right. Everett suddenly said, "But that's the way it's always been. Good people fight God's way, and bad people fight any way they want. But God helps the good people win."

"Then why haven't we won?" D.G. asked.

It was the question that dragged at Everett's heart, too.

If God really was going to help them, why hadn't He done anything? Why had it only gotten worse?

"Look," D.G. said. "Seth says God'll work. Well, all right, I'll buy that. But maybe the way God will work is by us doing the best we can with what we have. God didn't make Goliath lie down and kiss David's feet. David had to kill him. The walls of Jericho had to fall down. Abraham, Moses, all of them—God did some pretty amazing things. So how do we know that God isn't telling us to do exactly what I'm suggesting? Do you think He wants us to lie down and play dead?"

"No," Everett protested. "But maybe there's something else we can try?"

"Then what?" D.G. said with frustration. "Name it and we'll try it."

Fighting for a thought, nothing came. Everett sighed. "I just don't know."

There was a long silence. Then D.G. said, "All right, look at it this way. If God is really there and He can help us, then He's going to help us somehow. If He wants to override what we're doing, He can. If He wants to stop us, He can. Remember, it's not like we're going after Chuck Davis. He's coming after us. So it seems to me it's up to God to stop him, not us. We're the innocent party here."

D.G. piled argument upon argument. There was no way around it, at least at the moment. If God really could help, then He could do that regardless of what they did. Even if they made a mistake, couldn't God make it right?

Everett felt confused, and he could tell Tina felt somewhat like him. But in the end, what could they do but do their best and hope God made it turn out right?

Sometimes Everett wished he could run home and forget all of it. Just go into his room and play with his little plastic men, watch TV, and forget the rest of the world existed.

But he couldn't. He wanted to be a part of it. He wanted the tree fort. He wanted the fun. He wanted friends. He couldn't go through life running from everybody who threatened him, could he? D.G. was looking at them all thoughtfully. Finally, he said, "All we can do is try."

They all agreed.

Everett looked up hopefully. But somehow he knew there would be a fight. A real fight. A bad fight. Somebody would have to get hurt really bad before anyone stopped. That was the only thing that stopped them, wasn't it? Someone hurt and busted up and in pain. That was where it all led. Someone broken and bleeding on the ground.

He looked off into the woods, listening for the crack of a stick, the explosion of a party popper. But the woods were quiet. He wished it would hurry up and be over with.

20
The Con Job

Everett and D.G. worked on a way of running into Chuck and Stuart the day after Chuck got home. They were wearing camera equipment and had the newspaper clippings of the news about the Jersey Buckwolf sightings. Monday morning they finally crossed paths.

"Where are you going, Scarface?" Chuck called as Everett and D.G. passed by in the street.

Hurriedly, D.G. explained about the sightings and how they were setting up a "shot" down near the caves. Chuck examined the articles with interest. "I didn't see these," he said, though he nodded when D.G. showed him the one he'd cut out over a month ago. "Yeah, we clipped that one. You really think he's down there?"

"We're going to find out," D.G. said. "Setting up tonight. If you want to come by . . ."

"I don't know," Chuck said, squinting at D.G. Everett sensed Chuck was slightly suspicious.

"Anyway, we'll be down there about nine o'clock," D.G. said as they walked away. "It would be a lot less scary to have some others there."

"Yeah, well, we'll think about it," Chuck answered. As Everett and D.G. walked away, they heard Chuck begin talking excitedly to Stuart.

"Think it took?" D.G. said when they were far away.

"I think he's real interested," Everett said, his heart still bumping hard.

Monday night, they managed to come up with logical reasons to stay out late at the tree fort. They had flashlights, a tent, a camera, and their slingshots.

When eight-thirty arrived, long shadows and growing twilight left the woods in an eerie darkness. D.G. scrutinized his glow-dial watch and worried that Chuck might not arrive in time. Everyone was ready. The woods remained silent, except for the scurrying rustles of chipmunks and squirrels, distant dog barks, and the buzzing of mosquitoes. Even the stink of the skunk cabbage disappeared in the cool air.

D.G. and Everett waited in front of the tent, talking

quietly and listening frantically for the sound of Chuck or anything else in the woods.

"Do you suppose he would remember where to find it?" D.G. whispered.

Instantly, Everett saw the huge hole in all their plans. What if Chuck didn't? It was getting dark. Even with the moon beginning to poke through the trees, the quiet made every sound jump out at them.

Then they heard it. Voices. Sticks cracking. Two flashlights.

"Who's there?" D.G. called.

Silence.

"Who's there?" he yelled again.

"The Jersey Buckwolf." Chuck's voice. Close.

They stepped out into the little clearing. "Just came to keep you company, boys," Chuck said. D.G. shone the flashlight in his and Stuart's faces.

"We decided we wanted to be famous with you." He grinned at Stuart.

But Stuart looked terrified. His hard eyes and black hair looked even more sinister in the darkness, but he was obviously afraid. The woods, as the sun disappeared in the west, became increasingly eerie. The darkness seemed to surround them and move in until they were cramped into a tiny space around the beam of their flashlights.

They sat and talked for a few more minutes, then D.G. said, "If you're going to be a part of this, Chuck, you have to be quiet. We have to listen intently. Then catch it in the beam of our flashlight."

"How do you know it won't hack your head off, Scarface?" Chuck asked.

D.G. gazed at him. They were nearing a time when they could barely see each other. "That's the chance we're taking. We have a camera."

"So do I," Chuck said. "To take a picture of your terrified butts." He laughed, and Stuart snickered with him. Then they stopped talking and listened through the darkness. The moon was barely visible out above the creek. A few stars dribbled light through the leafy ceiling. Occasionally a branch rustled or something scampered by. Even knowing what should happen cranked Everett's juices to boiling point. He waited for that first noise on the tape. He only hoped Linc would wait long enough.

Minutes lumbered by. They sat for over a half hour in the quiet. The stillness of the woods was getting to everyone. Even Everett felt fear prickle up and down his neck and back. What if something else showed up—something they hadn't planned on?

Then Everett heard a distant click. He knew it sounded exactly like a tape recorder, but Chuck said, "What was that?"

D.G. whispered, "Shhhhh. We have to hear."

Chuck was more nervous than he let on.

The first eerie call came on the tape. A low, whistling, wind sound. *Keeeeeeee.*

Chuck moved into a crouch.

Holding up a hand, D.G. said, "Don't turn on your flashlight."

Chuck hissed, "I'll turn it on when I want to, jerk."

The *keeeeeeee* changed to a series of clicks. Louder. Like something was approaching.

"What is it?" Chuck whispered. His voice was tight. Everett squatted nervously, fingering the flashlight.

Then there was a rushing sound on the other side of the forest, where Tina was. Everything was going according to plan. The rushing sound suddenly stopped and everything became dead quiet. Both tape recorders were in perfect sync.

Then a cry with a series of clicks behind resounded from both sides of the forest. It was almost a howl. Almost a wail. *Hmmmmmmmmm!*

Chuck jumped up. So did D.G., Stuart, and then Everett. "Don't turn them on. Not yet," D.G. said. "We have to be cool."

"Be cool?" Chuck seethed. "Who are you kidding?"

More clicks. More cries. It sounded as if it was all over the forest. How D.G. had planned all this, Everett didn't know. It was great. If he didn't know what was happening, he'd have wet his pants and run howling from the forest.

The sounds seemed to close in. D.G. said one more time, "Hold off the flashlights. We're going to see something. We are. I know it."

Chuck looked stiff as a tile. "You don't think it'll kill us?"

"Just be cool," D.G. said. "Be real cool."

The tapes began the whispers D.G. had said were in Russian. It sounded guttural, unreal, terrifying. The tapes echoed back and forth.

"There's more than one of them," Chuck said.

"We better get out of here," D.G. cried.

Chuck clicked on his flashlight and shone it into the woods. Immediately the eyes lit up. "They're all around us." he cried.

It was time. The tapes were in sync. Any second now.

D.G. clicked on his light at exactly the place where the deer head was supposed to be. Two brownish blue eyes lit up. Then the horns. The black face. Tina moved it forward on ropes. The blue eyes around them seemed to crowd in on them. The whispered Russian grew louder. Then a deep guttural cry. "*Gettttttt themmmmmm! Getttttttt themmmmmmmmmm!*"

There was a horror-stricken pause. Then D.G. yelled, "Run!"

Chuck whipped around. They all sprinted for the creek. The woods seemed to crash around them. The tape recorders cranked up and the noises were louder. Chuck and Stuart howled.

The four of them sprinted through the woods, yelling and shouting, tripping over roots, scraping on brambles. When they reached the creek, all four jumped in and waded across. On the other side, they hurried up the hill till they were in the shadow of the Wattersons' house. They careened around the corner and ran into the street. Under a streetlight, they all stopped and panted.

"It almost had us," Chuck cried. "Did you get a picture?"

D.G. shook his head. "One. I don't know whether it even came out."

"I've gotta tell my dad," Chuck said. "He'll go crazy. Maybe he'll come down with his gun. I'm gonna call the newspaper."

Suddenly, Everett froze. Call the newspaper? That could really blow it. "Let us call the person," he said suddenly. "We already talked to him."

"No," Chuck said with a nasty gesture. "I know his name. I'm calling."

As he and Stuart headed off down the road. "You guys aren't so dumb after all," he called to D.G. as they walked away. "We'll all be in the papers."

As the two staggered off into the distance, D.G. giggled. He and Everett ran back behind Linc and Tina's house, crossed the creek, and found Linc and Tina at the tree fort. They told them everything. Everyone laughed and shouted.

"We did it!" D.G. suddenly cried. "We got them. They'll never be back."

Everett sighed with relief. How did D.G. do it? Maybe they had scared them out of the woods for good! Maybe the tree fort gang really was safe!

For the next two days, they heard nothing from Chuck or anyone else.

The foursome remained on defensive alert—ODA—as D.G. called it. Everett himself was astonished that it had all come off that easily.

They spent time hiding the peashooters and other weapons just in case. Everett watched with some fear as D.G. personally placed two A-bombs—the ammonia—in special spots, one in among some roots behind the tree fort, and another in the woods near the pile of extra wood. He resolved to ask his mother about it. Just to calm himself.

"What do you want to know about ammonia for?" his mother asked that evening as he sat before dinner fidgeting at the table.

"It's for cleaning and stuff, right?" he said, trying to veer off from any mention of D.G.'s use of it.

"I've used it many times. It does the job."

"Did you ever get any in your eyes?"

"Of course not. You have to be careful with it." She turned over some hamburgers in the frying pan and checked the green beans. That didn't sound so bad. People used soap all the time.

"But if you got some on you, it would be all right?"

She turned to face Everett. "Did you get some ammonia on you or something?"

"No, Mom, I'm okay. I was just asking."

"Well, don't play with ammonia," she said, turning back to the stove. "It's not a toy. It can burn your skin. And if it does get into your eyes, I think it could blind you permanently if you don't wash it out right away."

Everett swallowed. "But if you washed it out right away, you'd be all right."

His mother stopped and gazed at him again. "You're not using ammonia for something, are you? Not down at that tree fort?"

"Mom, I was just asking." As long as he didn't say no, he wasn't lying—at least he hoped he wasn't. But he didn't feel right about it at all.

She squinted at him. "Are you sure?"

"It's no big deal." He got up and walked out of the kitchen.

"I hope none of you are using ammonia as a weapon or something," she called after him. "It's extremely dangerous. You hear me?"

Everett answered, "Yes, Mom, I hear you." He went up to his bedroom and kicked the door open. "What am I going to do?" he murmured. "What am I going to do?"

The next morning he talked to D.G. about it one more time. D.G. assured him it would only be used in a last resort, and only with ample warning. "Don't worry," he said. "Chuck's probably too afraid to come back anyway."

Everett hoped again that the Jersey Buckwolf thing really had worked.

Things continued without a problem until Thursday. Then that evening after dinner, the foursome were all sitting on the top tier of the fort when they heard cracking sticks and leaf shuffling in the woods.

D.G. hustled everyone into position. "Let me do the talking, if it's Chuck. I'll find out what he wants."

Tina climbed to the top floor with a slingshot and got the pull strings for the net ready. Linc stood on the first floor with a sling, the water balloons, and eggs. Everett had a water balloon in one hand and an egg in the other. His sling was in his back pocket. Everyone had agreed no stones unless it was really bad. The peashooters and A-bomb were all safely hidden.

Everett and D.G. dropped to the ground under the tree fort. Everett's heart raced unevenly, jolting with great thumps at every sound in the woods. The cracking and brushing through the trees grew nearer. Then they spotted Chuck along with his four friends. They didn't seem to have any weapons.

"Well, well, what do you know?" Chuck's voice dripped with sarcasm. "The little ghetto gathers again."

D.G. stepped forward. His black eye had healed, but with his birthmark and dark features he looked ready for battle. "You have no business here, Chuck."

"Oh, I have all the business in the world." Chuck snickered and his four friends chuckled with him.

"We're giving you two warnings," D.G. said confidently. "Then it all breaks loose. Only two warnings. This is the first one."

Chuck stood there surveying the scene. He turned to his four friends and whispered something. They spread out to the right and left of him. "We came here to rid these woods of unnecessary structures," said Chuck. "In other words, we're going to knock down this heap for the sake of nature and ecology."

Stepping out in front, D.G. said, "We can't let you do that. So just go back and nothing will happen. But if you attack, we'll have to take punitive measures."

"Punitive measures!" snorted Chuck. He turned to the other four and leered. "Hear that? He's already sounding like a lawyer." He turned back to D.G. "Come to think of it, the only one I want is you, Frankl. Forget the fort. I'd just like to take you apart. We found out about your little Jersey Buckwolf job."

Everett knew there was no stopping Chuck now. He whispered up to Tina. "Go get Seth. I think this time we need him."

Tina didn't move. Everett said again, "It's our only chance. Get Seth." Linc nodded to her and she hustled out of the tree fort and onto the ground, then hurried off in the direction of Seth's house.

"Is that how you did it?" Chuck said accusingly. "With those Dobermans? Yeah, probably. You must think you're a real movie director, don't you, Frankl? They're all Jewish too, aren't they?"

"I don't know what you're talking about," D.G. said, glancing back at Everett. His birthmark was flaming.

"Sure you do." Chuck stepped forward menacingly. "You set us up. We went back into the woods to the cave. Found your little eyes painted on trees and leaves all over the woods. Pretty clever, Scarface. I suppose you got special effects on tape recorders or something, too. Always knew you Jews were clever. That's what my grandfather says. 'Jews is smart,' he says. Yeah, you got me the other night, Scarface. But you're not getting me again."

D.G. straightened up and glanced at Everett. He whispered, "Let me just stall him a little." Everett's heart was so loud, he thought he would explode. D.G. turned back to Chuck. "All right, then it's just you and me.

Whoever wins gets everything. We'll go. But we have to do it on equal terms. Fair and square. None of your guys get involved in this. Just you and me. It'll be a contest. Whoever scores the first three hits wins."

"Three hits of what?" said Chuck, a sly look in his eyes.

"Eggs," said D.G. "They're in these plastic eggs. I'll give you five and I'll take five."

Chuck smiled craftily. "What—I get to heave them at you?"

Suddenly Everett realized D.G. was winging it. Undoubtedly he understood what Tina was sent to do. If she came back with Seth and the dogs, most likely no one would fight. It would be over.

"But whoever scores three hits first wins," D.G. was saying, looking back at Everett and winking. "That's the end of it. Whoever loses, goes."

D.G. was just trying to buy time until Tina came back with Seth. He was fast, and Chuck was slow. It might work. Everett called up to Linc, "Get on the third floor and be ready."

Linc nodded and climbed up.

Curling his lips angrily, Chuck said, "Leave it to a Jew to make the rules." He turned to his four friends and they grinned. He looked back at D.G. "All right. Have your lackey there bring over five of them."

D.G. turned to Everett and nodded. "Just buying time," he whispered. But Everett realized if they—if D.G.—lost this, it was over for all of them. He quickly gathered up five plastic eggs from the stash and gave them to Chuck. The bigger boy took them with a sneer. Everett said, "Don't get dirty, Chuck."

"I'll get what I want when I want." He spat the words at him like BBs.

As Everett walked back, he told himself he'd make sure D.G. didn't get hurt. So long as it was just a contest, everything would be all right. Until Seth got there. *Just get them here*, he prayed in his mind. *Just get them here, Lord!*

Chuck laid the eggs on the ground. "No disturbing them," he said. "Sure you want me to turn you into an omelet, Scarface?"

Picking up two eggs, D.G. pranced back and forth warily. As Everett walked by, he said to D.G., "Just be careful. I'll back you up." D.G. nodded. He walked closer to the muck pit.

Everett took a position behind D.G. by the ammunition dump of colored eggs. He fingered his slingshot and waited. D.G. danced back and forth opposite Chuck. Each had two eggs in their hands. The bigger boy seemed nervous and fidgeted, jumping around every time D.G. stopped. Then D.G. pulled out his slingshot.

"Hey, that's not fair," shouted Chuck.

"Not fair?" answered D.G. "You can throw them a lot faster than I can load and fire. Besides, I have to be in a good position to shoot. I think you have everything on your side—if you're good with your arm."

Chuck sneered, "I can whip 'em pretty good."

"Then let's see what you can do. Take a shot. I won't move my feet."

Chuck shook his head and laughed. "I'm not falling for that. You just want me to waste an egg."

"Do what you want. But one thing I should tell you. Between you and me there's a little pit. If you try to come over on my side, you'll sink into it."

With sudden fear in his eyes, Chuck edged back and stared at the ground.

The moment he did, D.G. loaded his slingshot and began whirling it around his head. "Watch out!" yelled a red-haired boy, standing back by the trees.

It was too late. D.G. caught Chuck in the leg. The egg splattered on his pants, the plastic rolling off onto the ground. Linc cheered from the tree fort.

"You little dirtball," yelled Chuck. "Caught me off guard. You won't catch me like that again." He stooped down and rubbed the dirt, playing with it. D.G. began to load.

Instantly, Chuck was on his feet. He hurled an egg sidearm. It struck D.G. in the thigh and shattered off onto the ground.

"One to one," said D.G. with a smile. He leaped forward, trying to draw fire. Chuck instinctively moved back. D.G. whirled the egg around his head and pretended to release it. Chuck ducked twice, then felt foolish. Then D.G. ran forward quickly and stopped. Chuck stood his ground and threw a second egg. It was aimed at D.G.'s head, but D.G. ducked, and the egg ricocheted into the woods and cracked open.

"A dead one," said D.G. "You have three more."

He stepped back and watched Chuck pace. He began a slow whirl around his head. Chuck paced, ducked twice. In the middle of his second duck, D.G. released the egg.

Chuck danced out of the way, laughing. "Ha, you're not so good."

D.G. said nothing, but backed up over to the ammo pile and picked up two more eggs, all the while watching Chuck.

"He's not bad," whispered Everett.

D.G. nodded, his eyes fixed on Chuck. Then he ran to the left, his sling whirling. "Watch out, Chuckie, my man. This one's coming for your throat." He released the egg. It went cockeyed, ten feet off to the right.

"Two dead ones," Chuck called. "Now you'll have to hit the next two clean."

D.G. stooped down, writing with his fingers on the dirt. He drew an arrow. A moment later, D.G. stood, then bent down again and Xed out the arrow.

"What's that?" said Chuck. "Love letters for your girlfriend?"

"No, just getting the aim right."

D.G. stayed stooped on the ground. Everett waited, his heart booming through his ears. This wasn't nearly as bad as he expected. He kept looking over his shoulder for Tina and Seth. As Chuck roamed the other side of the muck pit, he dipped a toe here and there, trying to gauge its length and breadth. D.G. stayed put. Then he swung the sling and hit Chuck's hip as he tried to avoid it.

"Two hits," yelled D.G. "Just one more and I win."

"We'll see about that," Chuck muttered. He bent down, feeling on the ground. He stood and threw something. It wasn't an egg but a hunk of wood. He almost missed D.G. But it struck him on the heel as he spun out of the way. Chuck laughed.

"It doesn't count," shouted D.G., his face red. "Only eggs in this. It doesn't count."

Chuck shook his head. "Who's making the rules here, Frankl—you or me? I say it counts."

"No way," D.G. asserted again.

Chuck turned to the other four. "It counts, right?"

They all nodded like programmed robots. Then the four boys spread out behind Chuck as he laughed. He turned and smiled, giving them a thumbs-up.

D.G. and Chuck continued to jump and feint, trying to draw fire. Then with a yell, Chuck ran forward at D.G. D.G. backed up and tripped.

The moment he was down, Chuck threw his fourth egg. It struck D.G. on the side of the head, breaking open. His hair was spattered with egg yolk and white.

"Two!" Chuck shouted.

Before he finished his yell, though, D.G. popped up, whirling his last egg. Chuck was off guard and tried to back up. He was caught. Just as D.G. released his last egg, Chuck threw his in a desperate thrust. D.G.'s egg struck Chuck with full force in the chest. It splattered all over his shirt and his face. Chuck's egg sailed listlessly over D.G.'s head and clunked to the ground.

D.G. smiled. "Okay, now you can go. I won, three to two."

Immediately, Chuck bunched his fist and wheeled around to look at his four friends. Then he swiveled back around, a nasty sneer on his face. "No way, Scarface. I'm going to take you apart."

22 All Out

Everett steeled himself. He shouted to D.G. to get into the tree fort, but D.G. waved him off. Chuck picked up a rock. "Come on, Frankl, bleed."

Backing up, D.G. caught a root and tripped. Chuck threw the rock as hard as he could at D.G. It struck him in the thigh. D.G. rolled and jumped up, limping.

Bolting forward, Everett yelled at Chuck to stop it, to get out, it was over. But Chuck threw a rock directly at Everett's chest. It struck him in the breastbone and he fell down, wincing with pain and breathing hard.

A moment later, D.G. screamed at Chuck to lay off.

The other four boys hadn't moved. Chuck edged forward, peering at the ground, trying to figure out where the muck pit was. He slipped into one of the smaller holes, sinking six inches into the black, stinking goo.

D.G. limped over to the left side of the pit and put another egg in his sling. Everett knew this one had dye in it.

"Eggs don't count anymore," yelled Chuck. His face was red. He pulled his leg out of the pit.

D.G. began whirling the sling. "You like your clothes, Chuck? Well, this one's for your mother's laundry."

The egg splatted at Chuck's feet, sending inky black dye all over his white socks, sneakers, and legs. Everett could see Chuck would never let up now. His chest still hurt, but he got up off the ground and yelled to both of them to stop it. "Someone's going to get hurt. There's no point anymore."

"You're right someone's gonna get hurt," Chuck screamed. "And it'll be Frankl, one, two, three."

Tearing out his belt, Chuck roared, "Let's see what you can do with this, Frankl." He bounded around the pit and sprinted after D.G. The sling would be no good at short range.

As the four other boys started to run around the pit, Everett called up to Linc. "The net! Drop it!" Linc ripped the four strings.

The net cascaded down and caught three of them under it, including Stuart. They yelled, thrashing to get out. Only the red-haired boy was free. Everett held up a dye bomb. "Don't move," he shouted as he ran around the pit and herded the three caught boys toward it. "Come any closer, and I put this in your teeth."

Everett ordered them not to move. He had two dye eggs in his hands. "Linc has stones in the tree fort, and these are dye bombs. Move, and I throw."

D.G. now had one of the peashooters. Chuck pulled off his shirt and wiped the muck from his face. The dye, mixed with his sweat, came off easily. But D.G. yelled, "All right. That dye won't hurt you. But this will. This'll give you purple measles."

Chuck laughed, lashed the belt out again with a snap, and ran after D.G.

As D.G. blew the wad of powder out of the peashooter, the big boy screamed, and wiped at his eyes. With the sweat on his face, the dye turned a blazing purple instantly. Speckles appeared on his forehead, cheeks, and chest.

Weaving in and out among the trees, D.G. taunted Chuck, "That stuff doesn't come off, Chuck. You won't be able to go to the pool for two weeks."

Chuck stared at the purple specks. He looked like he had the measles. He wiped at them, but they didn't come off. "What is this junk?"

"It's used in catching shoplifters and thieves," D.G. shouted. He was reloading the peashooter. "Want to look like a pimple patch? Then keep on coming."

Chuck roared and barreled after D.G. The smaller boy

dipped and leapt around among the trees. Chuck caught him again in the arm with the belt and then on the cheek. Everett prayed desperately that Tina would show up with Seth. But no one appeared.

As D.G. fired two more bursts of powder into Chuck's face, angry, purple splotches appeared all over his chest, back, and face. D.G. was obviously too quick for Chuck.

As Stuart and the two others struggled to get out from under the net, Everett waved the dye bomb at them. Then with a growl, the red-haired boy leapt at Everett. Everett managed to jump aside, and Linc gave him a push. He ended up sitting in the muck pit. Immediately, Everett and Linc wrapped the net tighter around the other three and pushed them into it, too.

"Don't move," Everett screamed.

Chuck stood at the pile of boards near the tree fort. "See what you do with this, Frankl!" he bawled and picked up a long piece of wood with three ugly nails in the end.

It was way, way too far. Everett ran toward Chuck, yelling, "Put that down, Chuck. Put it DOWN!"

Chuck only laughed at him and waved it in his face. "Butt out, Abels." D.G. scrambled around behind them both looking for something. The ammonia? Everett blinked from D.G. to Chuck. He wasn't sure what to do. They were going to kill each other. That was where it was headed!

Swinging the stick menacingly in front of him with his right hand, Chuck turned back to D.G. The other boys had gotten out of the net now and were threatening to help

Chuck if Everett continued to interfere. Everett was caught in the middle now. He knew he couldn't stop Chuck and deal with the others at the same time. But somehow it had to stop. Where was Tina? And Seth?

He looked frantically for someone, anyone. But it was as if the rest of the world had simply vanished.

Everett watched helplessly as D.G. skirted between the trees, trying to defend against Chuck's stick. The bigger boy advanced on him, his stocky legs like stumps. His face was a mass of purple blotches. But not even that masked his anger and hatred.

Then something shrieked inside Everett's head, *You have to stop this*!

Both boys stepped into a clearing between two trees. Chuck drew the stick back and hurled it. It ricocheted off one of the trees and swiveled around, striking D.G. in the arm. He dropped to the ground for a second, panting, then jumped up and ran. "Somebody's going to get hurt, Chuck. Just quit."

"No way," the bigger boy screamed.

You've got to stop this, Everett! the inner voice shouted again inside Everett's head. He felt frozen in place, unable to move forward or back.

Stop this now before it's too late!

But Everett couldn't move. Again Stuart said, "You move, Everett, and we get into it."

Suddenly, D.G. and Chuck faced one another over the pile of boards. D.G. had his back to Everett and the others.

Both boys panted painfully. Chuck looked like something from outer space, with the muck, the purple blotches, and everything else. D.G. was bleeding at the shoulder and cheek.

Between rasps, D.G. said, "Okay, this has gone far enough, Davis, I think we should call it quits."

"You're just a coward, Scarface, that's all," Chuck wheezed in return.

But Everett could see they were both nowhere near finished. The voice resounded again, *You've got to stop this before it's too late!*

Everett stepped forward mechanically, heeding the voice. He knew he had to act. But a moment later, Stuart grabbed him at the shoulder. "One more time: This is between Chuck and Frankl."

Everett froze again, watching the two face off.

Slowly, Chuck pulled another board from the pile. D.G. cried, "You do that, and I'm going for your eyes with this."

D.G. had the ammonia bottle in his right hand. Everett's heart seemed to stop dead.

"I'm not kidding now," D.G. seethed. He brandished the bottle at Chuck and took off the cap. "You get this in your eyes, it'll blind you. I don't want to shoot any at you, but if you don't stop this now and leave, I will. I swear I will."

Laughing sarcastically, Chuck called, "Hear that, Stu? He's gonna let us go, unharmed." He glared at D.G. "And what about this, Scarface?" He pointed to the ugly purple blotches. "Who's going to pay for this?"

This time the voice in Everett's mind seemed to scream right through his bones, *You have to stop this. Now!* But he couldn't move. Stuart gripped his shoulders with his clawlike, steely fingers.

Chuck and D.G. dodged back and forth. The voice inside Everett's mind was deafening now. *Do something! Stop it! You have to stop it!*

He looked desperately off into the woods for Tina and Seth. Everyone stood around silently watching D.G. and Chuck, saying nothing.

It's not right! Act!

D.G. poured some of the ammonia onto the wood. Nothing happened, but D.G. yelled, "It'll burn bad, Chuck. Just go, and we'll forget this happened."

Chuck flailed the stick. "I'm not afraid of your ammonia stuff." He stepped forward, then suddenly he let the stick down. Chuck fixed his eyes on Everett.

The moment he did Everett felt an icy fear burst inside him. Chuck's eyes were filled with a hatred he'd never seen before. D.G. instinctively turned to look at Everett.

"No!" Everett screamed.

It was a trap.

The moment D.G. turned, Chuck leapt onto the pile of boards and jumped. D.G. was caught. He fell, then rolled to the right and stood up. The ammonia bottle dropped to the ground, dribbling its contents. As D.G. tried to wriggle away, Chuck clinched him at the ankle.

Pinning him with his hands, Chuck looked at the

ammonia and grinned wickedly. "Maybe I'll pour it on your face, Frankl. How would you like that? Maybe it'll clean that scab off."

With one hand on D.G.'s face, he leaned over to pick up the bottle.

Do something NOW! the voice screamed inside Everett's mind.

Chuck held the ammonia up. "See how you like this, Scarface!"

D.G. closed his eyes.

Now!

With a roar of terror, Everett leapt at Chuck just as he heard the bark of a dog. He screamed, "Stop!" and knocked the ammonia out of Chuck's hand, falling between the two boys. Out of the corner of his eye, he saw Chuck swing at him, his hand still wrapped in the belt. The heavy steel buckle caught Everett in the jaw.

He spun.

Tried to keep from falling.

Then falling.

Forward.

Into the pile of wood.

The nails!

Everett's neck seemed to explode. Something hard and stiff bit into muscle. He rolled over, flailing at it. Whatever it was was choking him. Everything felt wet.

Somehow he opened his eyes. Chuck stood over him staring, his face contorted. "It's spurting," Chuck shrieked.

A second later, he turned and ran.

Everett moved his mouth to say, "Something bit me." But no words came.

He watched as D.G. bent over him. The small boy pressed Everett's neck. Then Everett heard D.G. shout, "It's his jugular."

The other four boys ran out after Chuck into the woods. Then suddenly Seth's big face hung over him. "It's gonna be all right. Just hold on, son. Let me hold it, D.G., with my kerchief." Everett felt Seth's thick fingers crush his neck.

As Everett looked into Seth's sharp, blue eyes, he tried to speak again, but nothing came.

Let me sleep, he tried to say. *Let me just rest. Just be still. Just for a minute.*

The ground felt soft under him. It wasn't bad at all lying there. The sun was shining down through the leaves. He felt Seth's breath on his face, and it reminded him of the leaves. Something with leaves.

Seth kept his rough hands on Everett's neck. His big hands seemed to wrap all the way around him. What was Seth doing here anyway? Wasn't he supposed to be at work?

And Tina! *Man, Tina*, Everett thought, *you really should have gotten here sooner. You missed everything.*

She was staring down at him, crying. It was like seeing her down a great, long tunnel.

And Seth's hand was so tight on his neck. Why was he pushing so hard? If Seth would just stop pushing so hard, he could fall asleep. The ground felt so warm under him. But on top it was cold. So cold.

Then his mom was there. What was she crying about? Those gray eyes. She bent over him, way up there at the top of the hole. What was he doing in this hole?

He gazed into his mother's eyes. She was saying something. *Please. Please. Please.* Was that what she was saying? *Don't cry, Mom. It'll be all right. I'm just sleepy, that's all. It's just a dream. Don't cry. But I'm so tired. Just let me sleep. Just for a minute. That's all.*

Everett closed his eyes and everything seem to go dark inside him.

When Everett woke up, everything looked white. He blinked. Everything was so white. Then he saw his mother in the chair next to his bed. "Mom?"

She jumped. "Everett." Then she burst into tears and touched his cheek lightly "Everett, you don't know how worried . . ."

She kissed him.

"What happened? Where am I?"

"In the hospital, dear. Dad just stepped out to get a coffee."

"What happened?"

She shook her head and brushed at her tears. "We thought you weren't going to make it, honey. If not for D.G. and Seth."

"But what happened?"

"You fell into that awful woodpile where the pieces of wood with the nails were, and a nail punctured your jugular vein."

He tried to remember. The fight. Then the ammonia bottle. He looked into her eyes and said earnestly, "Is everyone okay? Did Chuck wreck the tree fort?"

She shook her head and wiped at her tears. Then she pushed his hair back and kissed him again on the forehead. "Everything's okay now. That's all that matters."

His brain still felt fuzzy. The white room looked nice. There were some flowers on the desk. Pink and red ones.

"Is D.G. okay?"

His mother nodded. "Please don't talk, honey. You have to get your strength back."

He shook his head. "Chuck was really going to hurt him, Mom. I had to stop it. He was going to pour the ammonia right in D.G.'s face."

His mother shook her head. "We know, honey. Now, please, just rest."

She was wearing a sweater and her makeup was smeared. But her eyes were so gentle. He said, "You're sure everyone's okay?"

"Yes, everyone's all right. They're all safe at home."

Everett searched her eyes, then closed his. The bed felt

good. Then he remembered. His neck. Something had bitten his neck. He reached up with his right hand. There was a large bandage there.

"Something bit me, Mom. I'm really sorry. But I had to do something."

His mother sniffled and gripped his hand. "Just rest, honey."

A few minutes later, as he tried to put it all together, his father returned. Gradually, the pieces fell into place. Everett learned he'd only been in the hospital for a few hours. An ambulance had come and some paramedics took him out of the woods. First D.G. and then Seth had put pressure on his jugular vein to stop the bleeding until they got there.

"I guess I'd better thank them," Everett said.

His mother and father said there'd be plenty of time for that. Over the next two days in the hospital gradually it all became clear. At the end of the second day as Everett ate his lunch, he suddenly said, "What's going to happen now?"

"There's going to be a meeting, honey," his mother answered.

"A meeting?"

"All of the parents and kids. We've decided we have to do something about this problem. So after you get home, we're going to have a meeting at the school with a police officer."

"A police officer?"

"Don't worry. He just wants to talk to us. It'll be okay."

Inside, Everett felt afraid and worried. Would they take away the tree fort and everything? But he didn't want to ask.

He went home the next day.

At first, Everett had to stay in bed and rest. But he kept wondering about D.G. and Linc and Tina. His mother said Linc and Tina had come by, but he was always asleep. She hadn't seen D.G.

Everett hoped they weren't mad at him. Anyway, what was there to be mad about? His mother said if Seth and D.G. hadn't known to put pressure on that wound, he probably would have died—bled to death before the doctors could do anything.

He kept touching the huge bandage. It felt like a steel rod rammed up in there. He couldn't move. It hurt to twist his neck around. The doctor told him to try not to. It might pull the stitches out.

But it all seemed so peaceful. He wasn't even sure how many days went by. He liked it when his mom sat down on the bed and read to him. She read him stories each afternoon and evening. From the Bible. David and Goliath. Abraham and Isaac. Then from *Treasure Island* and *Black Beauty* and The Chronicles of Narnia and *The Hobbit*. Books he'd always liked. It was so nice just to be peaceful for a while. It seemed like it had been so long since he felt peaceful inside. What was it, though, that he'd been so worried about?

Something in his mind didn't seem to work right. Mom said it would be that way for a while.

At home he played in his room. School wasn't too far away. Sixth grade. He forgot what the date was. But it had been near August. Maybe it was August. Or September. He wasn't sure. He wondered if Linc and Tina would be there. And D.G.? Sometimes he couldn't remember too well about it all. But he knew they'd be there. He was sure they would. They always were. They were the best.

Then after a few days, his mom said he could go out and play. Linc and Tina came over and they played games—Monopoly, Boggle, Aggravation—in his backyard. The second day, Everett said, "Where's D.G.?"

Tina shook her head. "He hasn't come around."

"But why?"

"We don't know."

Linc looked helplessly at Everett. "We called him—four times. But each time his mother said he couldn't come to the phone."

Everett wanted to go to the tree fort, but his mother told him to stick to the yard. Things finally started to get clearer. He remembered Chuck and the fight. And D.G. Boy, D.G. could be tough. Sometimes he wished he was that tough.

Seth came by in his truck with the dogs. But he didn't ask about D.G.

By the first of the next week, Everett felt back to normal. Linc and Tina had been over every day. He tried to call D.G. several times, but his mother said he wasn't available. He was afraid he'd never see D.G. again. He and Linc and Tina talked about it, but none of them knew what to do.

Then they had the meeting. Everett's minister was there, and the priest from Linc and Tina's church, and D.G.'s rabbi, and several people from the other kids' churches. But the main person was the police officer, Lieutenant Johnsbury. Everett sensed he really cared about all of them. He talked about how there were many different ways to solve problems between people, but rarely did a fight like this help either side. He spoke directly to Chuck several times about learning to live with people even if they were different, and he spoke to D.G. about working more to make peace than war. He seemed to know all about everything that had gone on.

Then he turned to Everett. He said, "You didn't want anyone to fight, did you, son?"

Everett shook his head fervently. That was absolutely true.

"And you didn't want to see anyone hurt, right?"

"No, sir, I didn't."

"Do you think there was any way to solve this problem besides the way you all tried to solve it?"

He seemed to be asking the whole group, but he was looking at Everett. Finally, Tina raised her hand. "Maybe we should have asked you."

"Right," the officer said. "Or your parents, or someone

else who could come in and help you all make peace." The tall officer shook his head fervently. "Sometimes people in the situation need someone outside of it to help solve it. There's nothing wrong with getting help."

The officer commended Seth for trying to help the kids the way he did, and Seth said he just hadn't realized how serious the problem was. The officer nodded with understanding. "That's the way it often is when kids are involved."

Then the policeman picked up a Bible. "I know you all might not read the book the same way as me, but let me just read you a verse from Paul. It's in Romans. It says . . ." And he read, " 'Do not be overcome by evil, but overcome evil with good.' Folks, I want to encourage you to do good to each other. Even if you don't like some of your neighbors, you can still do good to them. And if you don't know how to solve a big problem, get someone outside of it involved. If you don't know anyone else, come to me." He gave everyone a little card with his name on it.

Then he said, "That's all. And if any of you think you should apologize to anyone else, do so."

He left the room and there was a long silence, then Everett's mom got up and went to Chuck's mom and hugged her. Soon, everyone was hugging and saying they were sorry. Even Chuck shook Everett's and D.G.'s hands. Everett sensed there would be no more fights with Chuck. He wasn't sure there'd be a new friendship either, but he figured he'd leave that up to time. And God.

D.G. and his parents left first. Everett thought something was still wrong. He wasn't sure what, and he didn't ask his parents on the way home. Everyone was very quiet. At bedtime both his mother and father prayed with him. Then everyone hugged again and his mother cried. But finally they left him to sleep.

He thought a long time about all that happened. He knew the one thing he had to do was talk to D.G. with Linc and Tina alone. He prayed that it would happen soon.

24 Four Trees—Together

The next day, Everett moped around the house until his mother finally said he could go down to the woods. He wasn't to get into any fights, though. And no slingshots. He nodded. That was all right by him.

He stopped at Linc and Tina's. They said they'd be down as soon as they finished cleaning up their rooms.

As he sauntered down to the tree fort, the old feelings were returning. He felt stronger, and his head was clear. He remembered everything vividly now and felt like his old self. He only prayed that D.G. would come back.

He swung across on the rope swing like an old pro. He

liked the swish and the feel of the air on his face. He still had the bandage on, and the stitches. His mother changed the bandage every day. He wasn't supposed to do anything rough. But he was allowed to go down to the tree fort. That was all that mattered.

No one was there. The net was still crumpled up over the muck pit. He walked around and noticed the blood around the woodpile. *Good grief*, he thought, *what a lot of blood*. That was all his? He instinctively felt his neck and touched the bandage. But it was all right. The doctor said nothing could shake it loose, so he didn't worry about it.

He climbed up the rope ladder and sat on the second floor, watching the forest, listening to the birds, the squirrels, and the chipmunks. It was a peaceful place. He could lie there and just drift. Think about all kinds of things. Imagine himself floating on a cloud. Pretend he was a skylark, and dive from two hundred feet up. He could see it all.

He wondered where Linc and Tina were, though. What was taking them so long? No one ever came down here alone like this.

Suddenly, he felt this incredible impulse to climb. He stood up and looked at the four trees. One of them was great for climbing. He'd never noticed it before. He grabbed a branch and started up. Up. Up. Branch after branch. He could see more and more of the forest. The creek. Linc and Tina's house. The rope swing.

He stood there on a high branch watching the wind

play in the trees. It seemed to blow the leaves around, like a hair dryer or something. He'd never noticed that before, either.

He looked up into the sky, bending his neck back. Was God really up there? "Are You really?" he asked. Something in his heart resounded and he knew God was there, with him, in him. He felt safe and happy inside. Then he thought maybe he should pray. But what about? He figured he should say he was sorry for fighting and he said that. Then he said, "Thanks for the tree fort, God. Thanks for saving my life."

His throat felt tight and he stood there a moment, letting the breeze brush his face. Then he climbed down. Maybe he ought to clean some of the mess up. It really didn't look very good. The net needed to be put back up. And the tree fort ladder just hung there. It wasn't supposed to be like that. He walked around the site, looking at things, kicking at stumps and tufts of ground.

Then he heard voices. It was Tina and Linc.

Tina spoke first. "Looks pretty bad, doesn't it?"

Everett nodded with a wry smile.

Linc said, "Our parents weren't going to let us come down here at all. But we said your mom let you, so . . ."

Everett grinned. "Leave it to my mom to get everyone straightened out."

"We haven't seen D.G. since the meeting," Tina said.

Everett nodded and looked up at the tree fort. "He'll be back."

There were tears in Tina's eyes and she looked away.

Everett suddenly felt tired inside and fearful. What if D.G. really didn't come back? But he said, "Why don't we all go sit in the tree fort?"

Linc nodded and Tina followed. They climbed up and sat down.

Everett said, "I don't think there'll be any more problems with Chuck."

"Yeah," Tina said. "I really liked that policeman."

Linc murmured. "He was great."

Tina was looking at Everett's neck. She hesitated. Then she said, "Did it hurt, Everett?"

"What?"

"Where the nail got you?"

Everett shook his head. "It wasn't bad. Just some stitches."

Tina looked at her hands. "We all felt really bad. We thought you might die or something."

Everett looked at her, astonished. His mother had said that, but it suddenly hit him. He really could have died!

Linc was looking at him again. "But you're okay now."

Everett nodded. There was a long silence.

Tina said, "I wish D.G. would come back."

A lump hardened again in Everett's throat. But he said, "He will. He told me that once you're friends you can never stop being friends, ever. Not when you're real friends. And we are."

"I remember," Tina said.

Then Linc said, "Maybe we ought to clean things up a little."

"Yeah," Everett answered.

They all climbed down. The three of them went over to the net and started pulling it out of the muck and leaves.

"We'll never get this up without D.G.," said Linc.

Then Everett heard something and he turned around. It was D.G. He stood there alone, on the edge of the clearing. He had on his RUTGERS T-shirt, his jeans shorts, and had a little bag in his hand. Everett didn't even think. He just ran. All of them did.

D.G. stood there, trying to smile that lopsided smile of his. His hair wasn't combed. As usual.

There were tears in his eyes. He said, "I thought you all might hate me."

No one even seemed to hear him as they crowded around him.

"Did you like the policeman?"

"Are your parents mad?"

"How come you haven't called?"

"Your rabbi was nice."

"Has anything else happened?"

The questions came so fast, D.G. couldn't seem to answer fast enough. "I just thought you would never want to see me again."

"But why?" Everett asked.

D.G. shrugged. "I don't know. Because I was all for fighting Chuck so bad. I should have listened to Seth." He wiped at his eyes. "I'm sorry. I'm really sorry."

Tina hugged him. "It's okay. We did what we could, like Seth said."

For a moment, Everett felt something untangling in his brain. He wasn't sure what it meant or what it was, but something had happened.

Then D.G. said, "It didn't happen the way we thought it should, but I guess that doesn't matter. Because now maybe things will be right. So maybe Seth was right."

Suddenly, Everett had it. "That's it," he cried. "Even with all the wrong things God still made it turn out right."

"How do you know it was God?" D.G. asked, gazing at Everett skeptically.

He struggled again in his mind. Finally he said, "I guess we don't know for sure. But I believe it was."

"So do I," said Tina emphatically. She looked at Linc and he nodded, too.

D.G. chewed his lip. "You all really think so, huh?"

"Yeah," Everett said with Linc and Tina. "What else could it be?"

"Yeah, but you almost died," D.G. answered again.

"I know," Everett said quietly with a little shrug. "But maybe God was protecting me from dying. And you from the ammonia. And all of us. Maybe . . . I don't know. Anyway, I'm just glad we're still all friends."

Smiling, D.G. said, "And what's the favorite thing friends do together?"

"Eat!" all three of the others exclaimed happily.

"Yeah, I brought some cupcakes. Four different kinds." He held up the bag.

Everyone laughed and took a pack from D.G. as he handed them out. "This is great," Everett said. "Did you ever notice how quiet the woods gets sometimes?"

"Like right now," Tina said, curling up with her arms wrapped around her legs. "It's eerie. Like the Jersey Buckwolf might show up any minute."

"Yeah, rowrrrrr!" D.G. roared and they all laughed.

As the four of them ate, Everett looked around at the happy faces. It was just the way it had always been, what he'd wanted all along. This was what mattered, what made it worth it all. Even the pain. He had it now, and it would never be taken away. Not by Chuck or anyone. Never.

Maybe that was the good God had done. Or maybe it was something else. Everett wasn't sure. He figured he didn't have to understand it as long as God did. But he knew one thing: he was with his friends again. And for the moment, fights, wars, and problems he couldn't solve seemed as far away as winter. That was enough for him.

For more fun and adventure, read

Project Cockroach

"We'll go down in Jefferson School history."

That's what Ben Anderson promises when he gets Josh to agree to his plan. And turning loose a horde of cockroaches in Mrs. Bannister's desk drawer does sound impressive. Josh knows what Wendell, his peculiar next-door neighbor and classmate, would say, but what would you expect from a kid who actually goes to the library in the summertime?

Josh's mom wants him to be a good student and stay out of trouble. His long-distance dad back in Woodview wants him to "have a good year." Wendell wants him to go to church. But Josh isn't sure that even God can help him find answers to the questions in his life. He just wants to make a few friends and fit into his new world . . . even if it means taking a risk or two.

You'll find this and other Josh McIntire books by ELAINE McEWAN at your local Christian bookstore:

Project Cockroach...............................ISBN 1-55513-357-6
The Best Defense................................ISBN 1-55513-358-4
Underground Hero.............................ISBN 0-7814-0113-5
Operation Garbage............................ISBN 0-7814-0121-6

Chariot Books™
David C. Cook Publishing Co.